U767
20

GW00514774

Carson fastened the necklace carefully round Kirstie's slender neck, pushed back her shimmering hair and gazed into the deep green of her eyes. He sighed.

'Saved by a beach boy,' he teased, his eyes narrowing.

She struggled to sit up, her hand flying to the cold fragments of coral. 'Is this my payment?' she burst out. 'Two pounds' worth?'

'I paid three,' he said.

'How dare you?' she snapped angrily. 'I suppose because you're my employer you think it gives you some sort of entertainment rights over me when we're delayed. Well, you're very much mistaken, Dr Black. It gives you no rights whatsoever!'

He was taken aback by her vehemence. 'You're mistaken, Kirstie. I wasn't asserting any rights. It was simply a normal male reaction on seeing a very beautiful woman in a very romantic situation.'

Stella Whitelaw's writing career began as a cub reporter on a local newspaper. She became one of the first and youngest women Chief Reporters in London. While bringing up her small children she had many short stories published in leading women's magazines. She is deeply interested in alternative medicines and is glad that her son, now a doctor and anaesthetist, has an open mind about them. A painful slipped disc has improved since practising the Alexander Technique daily. Her three beautiful long-haired cats inspired her six published cat books.

Previous Titles

AN EAGLE'S EYE
BAPTISM OF FIRE

To Pat Tayler, a dedicated
air ambulance Sister.

# THIS SAVAGE SKY

BY
STELLA WHITELAW

MILLS & BOON LIMITED
ETON HOUSE   18–24 PARADISE ROAD
RICHMOND   SURREY   TW9 1SR

All the characters in this book have no existence outside the imagination of the Author, and have no relation whatsoever to anyone bearing the same name or names. They are not even distantly inspired by any individual known or unknown to the Author, and all the incidents are pure invention.

All Rights Reserved. The text of this publication or any part thereof may not be reproduced or transmitted in any form or by any means, electronic or mechanical, including photocopying, recording, storage in an information retrieval system, or otherwise, without the written permission of the publisher.

This book is sold subject to the condition that it shall not, by way of trade or otherwise, be lent, resold, hired out or otherwise circulated without the prior consent of the publisher in any form of binding or cover other than that in which it is published and without a similar condition including this condition being imposed on the subsequent purchaser.

First published in Great Britain 1990
by Mills & Boon Limited

© Stella Whitelaw 1990

Australian copyright 1990
Philippine copyright 1990
This edition 1990

ISBN 0 263 76983 6

Set in 10 on 11½ pt Linotron Times
03-9009-50972
Typeset in Great Britain by Centracet, Cambridge
Made and printed in Great Britain

# CHAPTER ONE

KIRSTIE'S fingers closed over the letter in her pocket. The paper was crumpled and stained. She had read it many times, still unable to take in the news it held. Strange how shock could deaden feelings. As she knew only too well, it was nature's way of shielding the body from pain.

She could see the Taj Mahal shimmering below like an iridescent pearl beside the muddy brown of the river. She had not realised that the great shrine stood by a river, built high on the bank, its marble minarets like delicate fingers reaching towards her in the vast azure sky.

'The most beautiful and enduring monument to married love,' said the first officer, peering over her shoulder as he returned to the flight deck. 'Pity we shan't have time to look at it.'

'Married love?' said Kirstie with a wry smile. 'With the UK soaring divorce rates, we'll soon be needing a shrine in England to remind us of what it's all about.'

'Do I detect the voice of experience? You're not the marrying type. A dedicated, single-minded career woman, surely?'

Kirstie returned his smile, but the strain showed in her eyes. Before that New Year party at her parents' home in Cumbria she would have agreed with him. Marriage was not on her agenda. But then she met Sean O'Brien, a young sheep farmer, at the party, and before the clock chimed twelve her head was spinning from his attentions. He kissed her, very thoroughly, to

5

welcome in the New Year, and she returned to London with enough daydreams to keep her imagination fully occupied on the long flights ahead.

'This has been the most marvellous New Year of my life, Kirstie,' he enthused before she drove away the next morning. 'I'll never forget it. Take care, I'll be in touch.'

But instead of promised phone calls there was silence, and now she had a letter. Not from Sean O'Brien but from her younger sister, Kate.

Kirstie moved away from the cabin window as the seatbelt light flashed on. She sat down on the first right-hand seat and belted herself in. It still seemed strange not to have rows of passengers to check, that last-minute inspection as the plane flew earthwards, then the frantic dash to a crew seat before landing.

She looked round the cramped interior of the plane, mentally checking the equipment. Everything was secured for landing: oxygen cylinders, doctors' ventilation case and circulation case, nursing case, miniscope, Liteguard defibrillator, stretcher and the all-important vacuum mattress and suction pump. There was hardly room to move.

Kirstie felt the jolt and bump-bump of the wheels as the British Aerospace 125 executive jet touched down, heard the screaming reverse of the engines. Not a good landing, she thought, but perhaps the runway was in need of resurfacing.

The plane taxied to a point left of the airfield away from the passenger terminus. Kirstie could see a stream of passengers, the women in brightly coloured saris, filing across the tarmac to board an Air India jumbo.

The door from the flight deck opened, and the pilot, Captain Rushington, came through mopping his brow.

'No sign of the transport for you yet. You'd better get out for a breath of fresh air, Kirstie. The auxiliary power unit has broken down. It's going to boil in here with no air-conditioning running.'

As Kirstie went outside the aircraft on to the top step, the heat hit her in waves. The sun was blinding and she fumbled in her shoulder-bag for sunglasses. To come from a cold, wet April in England, straight to this heat, was such a contrast. It had been a bleak winter with no sign of spring.

Her heels sank into the melting tarmac as she walked across to the edge of the airfield. She saw the parched brown earth, felt a hot breeze blowing dust from the plain. The Taj had disappeared behind a curtain of tall dark green cypress trees, but a strong sweet scent of incense and blossom filled her nostrils.

She found a bench to sit on, waiting for the transport to take her to the hospital, but content to enjoy the sights and sounds of India, even if she had come all this way and couldn't see the Taj. And she was not going to spoil the moment with reading that letter again. Not that she needed to read it. . .she knew every word by heart.

Quite soon trickles of perspiration began to gather and run down her neck and inside her uniform. She undid the top button of the tight starched collar, then the next, dabbing her skin with a handkerchief. She shook out her fine, flyaway silvery hair, letting the breeze comb through the strands. She was getting hot, but she knew it would be even worse inside the plane. The flight crew were standing in the only shade available under the tail, chatting and waiting.

Kirstie had read the patient's file many times since the call out. They were to collect a Mr Carson Black and companion. The patient had a complicated foot fracture, and, although Kirstie had spoken on the telephone to the Indian doctor in charge, it had been impossible to make much sense of the conversation. Mr Black had insisted that an air ambulance came out for him immediately. He refused to wait for a place on a scheduled flight. He sounded an awkward patient.

Slowly she eased her feet out of her lace-up shoes and wriggled her toes in front of her. It was almost like being on holiday, only she was working and hadn't brought any luggage beyond a comb, a lipstick and a mini overnight bag.

The sun was making her sleepy and she let her eyes close, its rays dazzling on her eyelids. Perhaps Mr Carson Black had changed his mind. Perhaps he and the unnamed companion had decided to go on a scheduled flight from Delhi after all. Perhaps the HS-125 would be given clearance to stay overnight and she could hire a cycle-rickshaw boy to take her the few miles to see the Taj Mahal. She would like to see little Mumtaz Mahal's perfect tomb on its great marble pedestal, to see in its filigree of flowers and jewels the extent of a man's love for one woman.

'Wake up there, woman!'

A man's voice broke into her sleepy daydream. Kirstie started, nearly falling off the bench, unnerved by the barked word which echoed her thoughts. A man on crutches was standing over her. He was tall, brown-faced and swarthy, two days' dark stubble on a square jaw, electric-blue eyes staring down at her with displeasure.

Kirstie caught her breath. For a second she thought she was still dreaming and the great Mogul Emperor, the Shah Jahan, had actually appeared. But the jeans were twentieth-century, and the dominant stance of

the long legs in them. The man was full of unleashed
power, despite the crutches and the foot in a lumpy
plaster. She had never seen a man quite like him
before. He had a kind of presence that was nothing to
do with his height or his muscled strength. His face
was in profile as he looked impatiently towards the
waiting jet, and she noted the strong, bent nose and
deep lines etched from nose to mouth.

She smiled a little to herself. She knew a broken
nose when she saw one, and wondered how many
brawls this tough guy had been embroiled in. Perhaps
the injured foot was the result of another brawl.

He turned sharply and caught her inquisitive glance.
He pushed his longish, unkempt dark hair off his
forehead and leaned forward on his crutches.

'If you're the nurse with the air ambulance, then
you're a poor advertisement for the service—uniform
unbuttoned, half asleep, hair like a haystack.'

Kirstie was fully awake in an instant. She knew she
was dishevelled, but it was hardly her fault.

'It is a little hot, sir,' she said evenly, buttoning up
her uniform and tidying her hair. 'Somewhat different
from chilly London. Perhaps you've been away a long
time, sir?'

'A month,' he said.

Just as she thought. . .swanning it around the world.
No proper job, getting into trouble, but at least with
the right medical insurance to bail him out in an
emergency. 'Mr Black and companion? I was expecting to collect you from the Das-Elam hospital.'

'I got myself here,' he snapped. 'I wasn't waiting
any longer than necessary.'

'Come aboard, Mr Black. We'll get clearance for
take-off as soon as you're settled. Can I help you?'

He shot her a look of disgust. 'I can manage—I'm

not a complete cripple. Those damned fools put on the wrong plaster. I want this off pretty quick before it does any damage. I told them, but no one would listen.'

Kirstie assessed his condition quickly. He looked in good shape despite the dust and dirt, and the clumsy plaster on his right foot. She could see it was a poor job. But the body inside the crumpled shirt and jeans was lean and fit. She tried to ease her feet back into her shoes, but they had swollen in those few minutes in the hot sun. Somehow she forced her feet in and kept a straight face. She stood up, ready to escort her patient across to the waiting plane.

'Where's your companion?' Kirstie asked, anxious to get her prickly patient aboard.

'She's still in the taxi, in the back.'

So much for gallantry, thought Kirstie as she hurried over, every step agony. She wondered who she was going to have to cope with now. She went to open the door, but the metal handle was burning hot and she gasped aloud. Using her handkerchief, she managed to open the car door.

'Hello?' she said.

There was no one in the car, but on the back seat was a cardboard box with holes in the lid. The box was rocking and a small dark nose was sniffing at the holes.

'Good heavens!' exclaimed Kirstie. 'A dog.'

'Bring it over.' Carson Black shouted as he hobbled across the tarmac.

'Animals are against the rules.'

'We'll argue about that when we get back to England. Meanwhile perhaps you'll kindly carry the puppy on to the plane, Nurse.'

'Sister,' said Kirstie, seething.

'I wouldn't have known it,' he remarked pleasantly.

Kirstie shook her head. The man was odious. Animals were strictly not allowed and she had no intention of breaking the rules for any man, not even one as domineering as Mr Carson Black. She wrapped her handkerchief round her burnt fingers and went to help the patient up the boarding steps. The small executive jet had its own let-down steps.

But Carson Black was already halfway up, using the strength in his arms and broad shoulders to hump himself upward from step to step. He ducked his head to go inside the cabin.

Kirstie hesitated, aware of more perspiration dripping down her neck as the sun blazed into the ground. They could not just leave the puppy to die in the hot taxi. Indians were not known for making pets of animals; they had enough problems feeding themselves.

There had been a change of crew, and the new flight officer took Kirstie aside. 'You can bring the puppy,' he said to her surprise.

'But——'

'Explanations later.'

Kirstie picked up the box, which immediately started to wriggle and bounce. She carried it on board and stowed it carefully on the floor of the cabin under a seat. The captain was already in communication with the control tower, requesting take-off clearance. They never wasted any time in getting away from a commercial airport, especially a busy one. And Agra was busy with tourists from all over the world flying in and out.

She occupied herself with her duties, aware that she was being watched through narrowed eyes. Carson Black had lowered himself into the front seat, flaked out, his dark head against the spotless head-rest, his foot propped on a case of equipment. Now she was closer to him, taking his temperature, wrapping the cuff of the sphygmomanometer round his arm, Kirstie was able to assess his injuries more accurately. This was not an isolated broken bone in his foot. There were lurid abrasions on his arms and neck and bandaged lacerations that needed attention.

I think it would be quite safe for you to have a drink,' she said. 'It's a long flight back and a good twelve hours before any anaesthetic.'

'Scotch on the rocks,' he drawled.

'Coffee, tea or a soft drink,' she said primly. She went to the galley and made him a strong coffee and a cool squash. He was probably dehydrated. She remembered the puppy and put some water in a kidney dish.

The puppy was panting and thirsty. It gulped down the water with splashy enthusiasm, drops spilling all over its muzzle. It was a very ordinary brown mongrel with big ears and a short, bushy tail, but it had beautiful liquid brown eyes that pleaded with Kirstie for love and affection.

'Poor thirsty baby,' she whispered into the box.

'No talking to my dog without permission,' growled Carson Black, the first glimmer of a smile hovering near his mouth. 'She only understands Hindi.'

Kirstie looked up. 'What have you two been up to? This puppy is covered in cuts and bruises too.'

'We got into a fight. Can you do something for her?'

'I'm not a vet, but I can try. It should be a simple clean-up job. But you come first—you're the paying customer.'

'I'll live. Women and children first. Fix Rauza.'

'Rauza?' she queried.

'That's her name. I thought such a nondescript dog should have a beautiful name. Taj Bibi ka Rauza means the mausoleum of Mumtaz Mahal, the most beautiful building in the world.'

'Yes, it is, isn't it? Though I've only glimpsed it from the plane,' she said, washing her hands.

'You haven't seen it?'

Kirstie shook her head as she prepared a disposable tray: packets of Steriswabs, sachets of antiseptic, forceps, gallipot, sterile dressing pack, a syringe and needle, tetanus ampoule. Whatever Mr Black said, she was attending to him first.

'That's a pity,' he added with genuine regret in his voice, as she rolled up his sleeves. His arms were a mess. 'Everyone should see the Taj at least once. It's so unearthly, indescribable. It's hard to believe that human hands actually built it.'

Gently she swabbed at the lacerations, removing bits of grit and dirt, dropping old dressings into a bag. What had he been up to? The plane was taxiing slowly to the head of the runway, so take-off was imminent. She fastened his seatbelt and took the puppy's box on to her lap as she sat in the seat behind.

She tried not to stare at his strong brown neck and the way his shaggy hair tangled with his collar. His shoulders were straining at the cotton of his shirt, muscles restlessly moving either side of the head-rest as if easing the pain in his foot.

When she returned to tending his wounds, she was still disturbed and tried to shut her mind to the smoothness and sheen of his brown skin, concentrating on her work. Gently she removed his shirt, her fingers brushing the dark hair on his chest. He said nothing, which was a blessing as she knew her hands were not too steady. He was looking more relaxed now, less aggressive.

Whatever was the matter with her? She had seen

hundreds of naked men, but never one that had affected her so deeply. She cleared the tray away and washed her hands again.

'Why didn't they clean you up properly at the hospital where they set your foot?' she asked. 'Those bandages were filthy.'

'Shortage of staff. It was a rural clinic, not a hospital. They had hundreds of patients queueing up for treatment and hardly any equipment. I didn't fancy using their supplies, even if they had enough to spare.'

Kirstie reheated the percolator and served coffee to the crew. Everyone was dry and thirsty. She took the chance to brush her hair, tucking the loose swinging strands behind her ears to keep it tidy. She caught a glimpse of herself in the mirror. Her cheeks were flushed, but her dark hazel eyes looked less strained. It was strange when hours ago she had been so down, so despairing. That letter had blown her away. Now she knew her salvation. . .it was work. She had not thought of Sean once in the last hour. Work would be her cure.

She knew her colouring was unusual. . .that flyaway silvery-blonde hair with eyebrows and lashes that were a glossy dark brown. She smiled and looked away. They were a trade secret from her air-stewardess days.

'I have to fill in a form, Mr Black. Can you tell me exactly what happened, please?'

'What's your name?' he asked.

'Kirstie Duvall,' she said.

'Have you sharpened your scalpel, Sister Duvall?'

'This isn't a joke, Mr Black. I have to make a full report, or how else will the hospital know how to treat you?'

'With respect, I hope.'

'Naturally. Now where did this accident happen?'

Kirstie averted her eyes from the man's hands. They were strong, clever hands—not the hands of a thug. Dark hair shadowed his forearms, and she was very aware of the way it brushed his wrists. His hands were loosely clasped in his lap; he was relieved no doubt to be on his way home. She wondered what it would be like to be touched by those hands. . . Her skin shivered and she pushed the thought away. She had managed for years to steer clear of attractive men, but now suddenly she was finding her emotions difficult to control.

It must be the effect of the unrepentant Sean O'Brien. . . He had broken through a barrier and left her vulnerable, not caring, it seemed, how his behaviour had rocked her stability. The sooner she rebuilt the wall, the better.

'Not exactly an accident,' Carson Black told her. 'It was a rural village outside Agra—one of those ramshackle places almost left behind in time, apart from the sale of cola and the sound of Indian pop music. Women washing clothes at a well, cows and goats wandering about, cyclists wobbling along the lanes. I was walking through the village on my way from Agra, when I heard a commotion and came across a gang of boys stoning a puppy which they'd tied to a stake.'

She saw a muscle in his cheek tighten and he ran the tip of his tongue over his lower lip.

'Rauza?'

He nodded slowly. 'It was very nasty. The boys were not the usual type of Indian youth. They were different, more aggressive, and they didn't like their sport being interrupted by a foreigner. So they turned on me. While I was untying the puppy, they vented their annoyance on my back. A rather large lump of concrete landed on my foot. Not funny if you're only wearing light trainers.'

'You could have been killed,' said Kirstie, shocked.

'Rauza nearly was.'

'If that concrete had hit your head,' she went on.

'But it didn't.'

'You were very brave,' Kirstie said, trying to sound cool and detached, but she could imagine the scene in the village and the terror of the puppy. Her opinion of Carson Black shifted. He obviously cared about animals even if he found it difficult being polite to her.

She finished her notes, holding the pen awkwardly to avoid touching the burns on her fingers. His hand circled her wrist and she found herself being pulled back to his side.

'Let me look at that,' he said. Gently he turned her hand over. 'Ouch! How did you manage to get those burns?'

'The door-handle of the taxi,' she sighed. 'I didn't realise that the metal might be hot.'

'My fault—I should have warned you. It's something that you wouldn't think of coming straight from the chilly UK. Got some cold water on board? You should have immersed your fingers immediately, but it'll still help to reduce the pain.'

'I do know how to treat a simple burn,' she told him.

'Then get on with it. A nurse with burnt fingers is useless.'

'I'm going to give you a sedative now, Mr Black, so try to get some sleep, It's the best way to pass the long flight. The stretcher might look hard, but I'm assured it's very comfortable.'

'Care to test it?' he said.

'Not part of my duties, sir.'

'Pity.'

He allowed her to help him on to the padded

stretcher bed fixed along the other side of the cabin and swallowed the sedative; she removed his shoe and loosened his clothes, raising the injured foot. She would have to watch his foot carefully during the flight. He looked tired now; the fight was going out of him. His long dark lashes were fluttering as he fought against their heaviness. He needed a bath; he looked the kind of man who showered frequently.

She tidied away her equipment, automatically riding a slight patch of turbulence, and thought he had drifted off to sleep. But she was wrong.

'Cold water,' he murmured as she walked past.

The relief was immediate. Her fingers tingled as she plunged her hand into a small basin of cold water. She stood on one foot, then the other, wishing she could slip off her shoes.

She went through to the flight deck and asked the captain to turn up the temperature control as it was becoming chilly. Then she turned down the cabin lighting and hoped her two patients would sleep well. The puppy was curled round in her box, nose tucked into her paws, snoring lightly. Kirstie prepared a quick snack for the crew, then stretched herself out on the front seat to catch some rest.

The dimmed light was very soothing, the throb of the engine like a low lullaby. Kirstie could have fallen asleep, but did not allow herself to even doze. The patient was entirely her responsibility and, though Mr Black was not seriously ill, she still had to be alert for any change in his condition.

Thoughts of her sister came into mind. . . Kate as a bright youngster, fair plaits swinging as she jumped over a gate; Kate as a teenager learning to ride a bike; Kate going swimming with the latest boyfriend, going to dances, staying out late. . .

'You will come to our wedding, won't you?' Kate had written in her large, childish hand. 'It'll be in July. Sorry, I can't ask you to be a bridesmaid as Sean has three young cousins all desperate to wear long dresses. You met Sean at the New Year party, didn't you? So you'll know how wonderful he is and how happy I am to be marrying him.'

Kirstie smothered a hopeless sigh. It was her own fault. She could not blame Sean. It had been a lovely party with too much wine, too many uninhibited kisses. She must have been out of her mind to take him seriously. It had not meant anything more to Sean than an exciting encounter with a young woman from London, someone who lived too far away to see again.

She was the one who had read too much into Sean's attentions. All of a sudden she had wanted it to mean more. . .that close dancing against his body, cheek to cheek with his smooth boyish face, his eager mouth determined to show her that he knew how to kiss. It had been so romantic and stirred hidden responses in her body that were dangerous and unreliable.

Well, it would never happen again, she promised herself. She would make sure of that. She would not allow it.

She supposed she had been feeling particularly lonely that evening. Both during her early years of flying with British Airways, then the arduous training to be a nurse, she had found little spare time to visit her parents. She had made an effort that New Year and arrived at the party wearing all the surface gloss and glamour of an ex-stewardess.

But apart from Kate and her parents, she had not known a soul. Then Sean O'Brien had homed in on her, six feet of muscle and brawn, and barely left her side, dazzled no doubt by her sleek black dress,

flawless make-up and shimmering silver-blonde hair.
Sean had seemed so wholesome and young, skin
tanned by his outdoor life, his attention and admiration flattering.

What a fool she had been, carried away with wishful
thinking and daydreams like some love-struck teenager. She would know better than to let her emotions
get involved again.

Carson Black stirred and Kirstie went over to her
patient. He had thrown off the light blanket and was
stretched out in exhausted abandon, one arm behind
his head. His long dark lashes fluttered in dreaming,
but his muslces twitched as if they were more like
nightmares than pleasant dreams.

She gazed at the craggy planes of his face, lingering
on the strong, attractive features, observing that his
well-shaped mouth was fringed with perspiration. It
was not fair to look at him when he was asleep, a
stranger, a man she would not see again. Somehow
she felt she needed to look at him. Those first electric
moments would never happen again, so she had a right
to record on her brain the kind of man who could
cause those shock-waves.

Mentally she gave herself a shake. Young Sean and
now Carson Black! There must be something wrong
with her. The two men were so totally different, one
an exasperating, strikingly mature man, the other a
handsome, cheerful boy. It was time she took herself
firmly in hand and cut the male sex right out of her
life.

She paused as she returned to her seat. What could
be the cause of all her confusion? She had been so
busy with her careers that there had been little time
for a normal relationship with a man. Plenty of nice
men around, but never one that meant anything special

or stirred the deepest feelings in her heart. She had left no room for love, believing independence and work satisfaction to be more important.

Carson Black woke from his disturbed sleep but did not move. He listened to the steady engine throb and watched the lightening of the sky through a nearby cabin window. They were flying into dawn.

He heard a sigh and saw that Sister Duvall's slim shoulders were slumped in despair. For a moment he was puzzled by her look of fragile desolation. It worried him. What were her problems? Surely life must be one long party for such a pretty young woman, all that bobbed silvery hair framing a delicate face with a lovely, generous smile. He saw her shapely legs in sheer dark stockings and half smiled. No wonder she had been hot at Agra. The whole uniform was impractical for nursing aboard a plane and in different climates. He felt sure that, beneath that stiff navy dress, Sister Duvall's figure was trim and alluring.

He turned his mind back to his injured foot. The pain-killer was wearing off and his leg was aching. Damn those thoughtless boys, damn his own interference, damn the whole sequence of events that had brought him down just when he needed all his energy and drive.

Kirstie moved over to him, instantly alert. She checked the colour of his injured leg for any sign of blueness. At the first tinge she would be hacking off the plaster.

'It should have been bivalved,' she said.

'I tried to explain about allowing room for swelling or any pus to get out,' he told her. 'It should be split or a three-quarter plaster. I don't think they knew what I was talking about. I could lose my leg.'

'You were right to insist on an air ambulance,' said Kirstie.

'Thank you, Sister. I'm glad to gain your approval about something. And I need a plaster up to the knee to immobilise the ankle. This boot thing is useless.'

'Don't worry, you'll be getting a proper cast soon.'

'I'm very thirsty,' he murmured hopefully.

'I'll fix you a mouthwash,' she said. 'We'll be refuelling at Rome soon and then it'll only be a couple of hours before we reach London.'

She fetched some mouthwash and a bowl, her mind on the procedure for landing any minute, and was quite unprepared for what happened next. His free arm went round her neck and pulled her face down to his. He was strong and she did not have a chance, caught off balance close to the stretcher.

His mouth was warm and seeking, roving over her soft lips with delicate insistence at a deliberately lazy pace. Gently his lips teased hers open, nibbling, touching, tasting. His tongue sought the softness of her inner lips, exploring the flesh and moistness. Kirstie stifled a low moan of protest as the slow seduction caused a firestorm of sensations. She was mesmerised by the gentle probing, his mouth tasting of orange. She lost all sense of time and place. Her mind went blank, though somewhere it registered that this was adult kissing on a scale that she had never experienced before, and a million miles away from Sean's enthusiastic assault.

She was close to his breathing too, feeling the masculinity of his chest against her as it rose. The metal edge of the stretcher was hard against her thighs; it was the only touch of reality.

At long last his grip on her neck lessened and she was able to draw away, trembling. Her heart was pounding, making it difficult to think straight. His piercing blue eyes were glittering darkly as he observed her reaction.

'Better than a mouthwash, Sister,' he said, an unexpected tinge of regret in his voice. 'Not on the NHS.'

'How dare you?' she gasped, not understanding how he could just stop such beautiful kissing.

'Sit down and belt up,' he said laconically. 'We're about to land at Rome.'

Her fingers were trembling as she fastened the brace belt over his shoulders meeting the pair round his waist. The clasp was a big, cumbersome buckle, but it could be flicked open in a second in an emergency. She felt like strangling him, and gave the webbing an extra hard tug. A grin flashed across his face as if he understood.

'Sorry. Say it was my weakened state of mind,' he added as an excuse.

'Weakened state of mind, my foot,' she stormed in a low voice. 'Typical male arrogance.'

But she knew she would not have missed those few minutes of tenderness for a million pounds. The memory would never leave her. She supposed she ought to be grateful to Mr Carson Black for teaching her that such miraculous kisses existed, except that now she had found a standard that might be impossible ever to reach again.

The refuelling stop at Rome was brief. Kirstie took the opportunity to take Rauza for a quick walk outside on an improvised lead, hoping that no airport official saw her. She gave Carson Black another pain-killing injection, calculating that it should last until he reached hospital. She kept her distance, but he seemed preoccupied, the nearness of their destination bringing a normality into the cabin atmosphere.

Kirstie made more sandwiches and coffee for the crew after she had checked, stowed and secured the equipment; everything had to be ready for their next emergency flight. They could be called out again any time.

Kirstie had enjoyed being a stewardess and accepted the frantically hard work of each flight for the joy of flying and seeing the world. She might still have been cabin staff if a flight from New York had not suddenly escalated into a drama. A drama that came back with vivid detail, underlining her own helplessness to deal with the situation.

She fingered the fine white scar high on her left cheekbone beneath the swinging hair. It was her memento of the flight, though she hardly remembered the man who had dealt that stinging blow and whose heavy ring had slashed her skin.

'How's our patient?' asked the pilot, taking a coffee.

'A very forceful personality,' said Kirstie. 'A man who knows his own mind and manipulates everyone else.'

The pilot grinned. 'I'm not surprised. He has that reputation.'

'You know him?'

'I've heard of him. . .quite recently, in fact. He's an entrepreneur of sorts, tries his hand at different enterprises. I've seen his name mentioned on the City pages. He was involved in the take-over of a drug company some years back.'

'Sounds like him. I should think take-overs are just his scene. I doubt if humble pie is ever on the menu.'

'More like caviare and champagne. Over the English Channel now. We won't be long landing.'

'I'd better get back to Mr Black,' Kirstie said. 'Before he complains that I've been neglecting him.'

In her absence, the long-limbed man had climbed off the stretcher and struggled over to the seat, his plaster propped on a makeshift footstool. He was peering out of the cabin window, watching the tiny boats bobbing below on the sea.

'You should have waited for me,' said Kirstie, exasperated. 'Supposing you'd fallen?'

'You were too busy chatting up the pilot and I wanted to see where we were. The English Channel always gives me that coming-home feeling, even if I've only been away a few days. By the way, I want to thank you for looking after Rauza. Has she been good?'

'Very good. Though I'm not sure if ham for breakfast isn't against the Hindu faith.'

'Since I haven't determined her religion yet, I think we can safely assume that ham is OK.'

'I'm relieved about that,' said Kirstie. 'You do realise that this animal has to go into quarantine for six months, don't you? Or are you intending to smuggle her in under a hospital blanket?'

'I'm not that irresponsible,' Carson Black said fiercely. Although at that moment, with another night's growth of stubble on his chin, and his long dark hair a tangle of dust and sweat, he looked more like a pirate than a responsible citizen. He only needed an eyepatch and a cutlass. 'I have heard of rabies. I only look ignorant.'

Kirstie's reprimand dried up as suddenly she remembered the sensations roused by his searching kisses. She knew she was blushing and looked around, wondering what she could do to recover her composure.

'You're very slack on the seatbelt procedure,' he remarked, fixing the clasp himself. 'This is the second time you've nearly missed the sign.'

Kirstie choked on her retort. She could not be rude to a patient, though she longed to tell Mr Carson Black exactly what she thought of him. Instead she gave him a saccharine smile and went to another seat.

At Heathrow an ambulance was waiting to take Carson Black to hospital. Quarantine officials came on board with papers for him to sign prior to taking Rauza away to nearby kennels. Kirstie fondled the puppy's soft head.

'Off to your six months' solitary,' she said.

'Better than a death sentence,' said Carson Black icily.

'I'm sure you'll soon be out of pain and able to resume your travels in India, Mr Black,' she said in a tone of voice that implied that she hoped he would soon be as far away as possible.

'Thank you, Sister Duvall,' he said with equal coolness. 'For your. . .' he paused for effect '. . .delightfully expert co-operation.'

She knew what he meant and she was defenceless. She helped him down the steps, struggling with a fury and sudden unexpected sadness. Once she had delivered him to the hospital, she would never see him again. Neither a suave Indian prince, nor a bold dark pirate. It was just as well. . .she was not equipped to handle a pirate.

'I hope I never see him again,' she said through her teeth as the captain joined her. 'He's absolutely impossible.'

'Somehow I think you will,' he said, and he was chuckling. 'I forgot to tell you how it was I'd recently heard his name. He's your new chief medical officer and he's just bought the air-ambulance company you work for. I didn't tell you because I thought it might be somewhat offputting to know the real identity of your patient.'

Kirstie stood by the ambulance door, hollow-eyed and stunned by the news, gripping the door-handle with her burnt hand, not even feeling the raw pain.

'Sister Duvall,' Carson Black shouted. 'Stop gossiping. I think my leg's going blue.'

# CHAPTER TWO

'Come in. The door's open—no need to wait outside. This isn't a dragon's den.'

A pang of apprehension halted Kirstie as the deep tones of her new employer ordered her into his office. It was not an imposing place, two rooms over their stores warehouse on a trading estate. The office was situated between hangars on the perimeter of Heathrow International Airport, the flat, misty, foggy plain once called Hounslow Heath. She tried to feel calm and sensible, but she had never had to face an inquisition before.

One of the rooms was a fully equipped airline operations centre, the heart of the Air Ambulance Medical Service. They were an established company linked to a group of insurance companies who guaranteed an air-ambulance service to bring clients home in an emergency for medical treatment. The big commercial airlines also used the service on occasions when they had no aircraft or trained staff available.

Kirstie was glad she was wearing her own clothes— a snow-washed blue denim shirtwaister that looked neat and businesslike, the narrow belt emphasising her trim waist. Her canvas wedge shoes were smart and comfortable.

'Ah!' she said involuntarily as she went in.

Carson Black cleaned up was even more devastating than the pirate model. The stubborn jaw had been freshly shaved and revealed a slight cleft, and the unruly hair trimmed and shaped into the nape of his

neck. The absence of dirt and dust made the blue of
his eyes even more brilliant. He was wearing sharply
pressed grey trousers, a dazzling white and blue stiped
shirt and tailored navy waistcoat. A navy jacket was
slung over a chair.

She had a brief feeling of *déjà vu*. . .somewhere she
had seen this tall man before. She shook off the
feeling. Of course she had seen him before; that flight
back from Agra a week ago had been no daydream.

He was standing by the window watching the planes
taking off, the double-glazing dulling the shattering
noise. It wasn't until he moved that Kirstie remembered his injury.

'Sister Duvall—come in and sit down. You're late.'

'My car broke down,' she apologised. 'It's old and
accident-prone.'

'Not a very sensible vehicle to run. You need
something reliable in this business. Would you like
some coffee?'

'Yes, thank you, Dr Black, that would be nice.' She
did not offer to help as he hobbled over to a side-table
where a Cona percolator was bubbling. He was not
the kind of man who would appreciate assistance.
'How's your new plaster cast?' she asked politely.

'Excellent,' he said. 'No further damage to the foot,
I'm pleased to report, thanks to your superbly efficient
administrations on the flight home. Two metatarsal
fractures. The plaster will be off in five weeks—my
bones knit fast.'

Kirstie thought his comments were a wild exaggeration of the truth. It had been her normal routine care
of a patient, but she decided not to argue the point. If
Carson Black thought she had been marvellous, then
he could go on thinking it.

'You weren't so complimentary during the flight,' she reminded him.

'It was stress,' he said, handing her a cup of coffee with a devilish twinkle in his eyes. 'I was testing to see how you reacted with a difficult patient. I wanted to find out if you could cope.'

Kirstie nearly choked on the steaming coffee, longing to deflate his complacency with a stinging remark. 'I was sorely tempted to use handcuffs,' she murmured.

'You did very well. You kept your cool, and were in fact the perfect nurse on a very long flight. You were alert for any change and always available—no sloping off for a quick snooze at the back of the plane. I was also impressed with the way you looked after Rauza. You might have got into trouble for taking her for a walk.'

'It was all right, she was on a lead,' said Kirstie. 'I'm glad I passed the test. Perhaps you'll kindly warn me another time or I shall suspect every patient of being an undercover snooper. How is your puppy?' she added. 'Is she enjoying her incarceration in a foreign country?'

He sent her a sharp look across the well-polished walnut partner's desk which almost filled half of his office. 'I gather you don't approve of my bringing the puppy back to England, but she's healthier and happier in kennels than running wild and scrounging scraps in India. That is, if she'd survived the stoning.'

'I'm glad you're sure she's happier.'

'I've visited her twice and she came bounding over as if she really knew me.' He sounded as pleased as a child.

'How nice,' said Kirstie, wondering if he had asked her there just to talk about the puppy.

He was flipping through a file, and, though it was upside-down, she could read her own name on the top. It was not fair that he should know all about her and she should know nothing about him. She noticed there were strands of grey in his hair at the sides and a few in the untamed locks on his forehead. He was older than she thought, about thirty-six.

'I suppose you know that I've bought AAMS,' he said, not looking up. 'I want to meet all the staff personally and sound out my ideas for improvements.'

'Improvements? Are they needed? We've always prided ourselves on running an efficient service,' said Kirstie coolly.

'There's always room for improvement,' said Carson Black, taking a deep breath before he tackled a sensitive subject. 'Your uniform for a start. It's out of the ark and hopelessly impractical. Wouldn't you prefer something more comfortable and adaptable for working in? A starched collar and short skirt might be OK for a sister in a big teaching hospital, but it's hardly practicable for climbing in and out of planes.'

'A sister's uniform is traditional,' said Kirstie, when she could trust herself to speak. 'Or do you think a supermarket overall would be more suitable?'

'I'm not advocating that you should be as glamorous as an air hostess,' he said pointedly. 'Our image is not centred on the drinks trolley.'

Kirstie clamped her mouth shut. She was not going to be drawn into an argument, especially as he must know she had been a stewardess. Some people refused to take airline work seriously. It was all in her file, but not her reason for leaving and training as a nurse. There was no shame attached to her leaving BA; there had been a problem and she had dealt with it the best way she could.

He was watching her, summing her up, trying to fathom the character behind those dark tigerish hazel eyes and wide, curved mouth. He would have liked to get to know her better, realising she was both sensitive and intelligent, but there was no room for any such development in a business. Those kisses on the plane had been a mistake; he must have been light-headed from the cocktail of medication.

She too was remembering the slow, drugging kisses in the night hours that had devastated her. Had it really been the same man as this well-tailored, waistcoated business tycoon who regarded her imperturbably across the desk?

'What are you thinking, Sister?'

'I'm wondering why a medically qualified doctor is sitting behind a big desk, running a commercial company instead of saving lives in a hospital.'

She saw his mouth tighten and he snapped shut her file with a deliberation that was not lost on her.

'I could ask the same of you. Why aren't you nursing on a ward, putting in long hours and night duties instead of flying all over the world? Look at your qualifications—midwifery, intensive care, then inflight nursing.'

'I suppose air-ambulance work sounds attractive,' she retorted. 'But my hours are just as long, sometimes longer, with no relief at all, and unless a doctor flies out with me I have sole responsibility for the patient. And there's no shortage of night duty, I promise you. I'm trying to catch up on my sleep all the time.'

'I apologise, Kirstie,' he said, using her Christian name for the first time. 'I do know that being a flying angel isn't all candy-floss, and my job is not as commercially orientated as it might appear to you at first. True, AAMS desperately needs funds to back its cash flow. To be efficient it must be financially stable. But it's my ambition to build AAMS into a first-class, worldwide medical service, the envy of all airlines, providing the kind of medical back-up that will become more and more vital as travel expands. It's going to grow, Kirstie. Already people commute across the Atlantic——'

'Pop stars, soap stars,' Kirstie murmured.

'They're people too. And when they're taken ill or involved in an accident, they're very ordinary people, wanting to get home fast for the best treatment on offer.'

Kirstie calmed down. Carson Black did sound genuine in his determination and she also wanted people to have the best medical service available. The first hours of an emergency could be traumatic, and the only help available in a foreign country was sometimes chaotic. Patients were always so relieved and grateful when the air ambulance arrived.

She remembered her Sister Tutor saying, 'Your words and your smile are the patient's best medicine.'

'I think we both have the same aims at heart,' Carson Black went on more slowly, looking at her with an intenseness that made her uncomfortable. 'Patients deserve the best and fastest treatment. That's what I'm going to give them, a first-class organisation and a first-class medical team. I need someone like you, Kirstie, to help me organise it. I want a reliable sister to head my nursing team. Will you do it?'

He had stood up, and Kirstie's head was spinning. The office was run on a shift basis with two full-time nurses, herself and the redoubtable Lynda Marshall. The rest were freelance nurses and locums on call, but even with answering phones and bleepers contact was often delayed. She glanced up; somehow she had lost track of what he was saying. The only reality was the tallness of the man towering over her, the burning look in his eyes, the way he was draining her will-power.

She was saved from answering by the urgent ringing of the phone. It was the hot line. Carson Black picked up the phone and listened intently, making notes of names, phone numbers, foreign contacts.

'Right, I've got that. We'll ring you back to confirm all the arrangements. I'll get on to the aircraft brokers immediately and see what they have available.'

Carson went through into the adjoining operations room, putting into action the calls for hiring a plane, laying on transport at each end of the transfer, preparation for the hospital admittance. Kirstie had seen it all before, was always amazed how quickly everything could be arranged. She went to the filing cabinet and got out the necessary forms to start a new file. There were also equipment and supplies to indent from the stores.

'The mission is Venice,' said Carson Black. 'Who's available?'

'I am,' said Kirstie. 'I'm on duty. What's happened?'

'Fractured skull and chest injuries. A man fell in a canal and was crushed by a vaporetto.'

'A what?'

'It's a kind of water bus.'

'Sounds really bad.'

'I'm coming too. You'll need a doctor on this one.'

A heavy mist hung over the lagoon, a swirling grey wraith that hid the canals and palaces. Kirstie always hated fog, even after years of flying and automatic landings. She had checked all the equipment during the short flight out and everything was ready for their seriously injured patient.

Carson Black had spent the journey on the flight deck, talking to the pilot. He was using every minute to immerse himself in the technicalities of air brokerage.

'Marco Polo Airport,' he said, coming over to Kirstie. 'The weather report is cold and misty. You'll need a coat.'

Kirstie shivered. It did look chilly outside. She had changed into her uniform in the toilet on board. 'I haven't got one,' she said. 'I'll manage without.'

'Nonsense, you'll get frost-bite. Put this on.'

Carson pulled a big padded parka from the crew locker and draped it over her shoulders. She was lost in its baggy folds. He tucked her silvery bob inside the collar and touched her pale cheek with the tip of his finger, noticing the fine white scar for the first time.

'Snug as a bug,' he said lightly.

'Are they meeting us with an ambulance at the airport?' she asked.

'No, they can't get through because of the fog. A water taxi is waiting to take us to the hospice where the judge has been taken. We'll bring him back—it'll be quicker.'

'Judge? Is this one a VIP?'

'He just has a title that goes with the job.'

The water taxi was waiting at the flight of steps a short distance from the terminal buildings, water lapping against its hull. Carson took his medical bag from Kirstie and helped her into the rocking boat. The driver hardly gave her time to sit down before he let out the throttle and sped through the marshes to a channel through the lagoon. The channel was marked with black wooden piles, dark forbidding relics. The mist swirled round, closing the two of them into a spooky isolation. She sat next to Carson, aware of his profile, so strong and sharply defined, marred only by the kink of a broken nose.

'I don't think I'm going to see the palaces in the Grand Canal either,' she said.

'That's a pity,' he said with commiseration. 'The *palazzi* are so beautiful. You should see the Grand Canal, all these fantastic *palazzi* built on either side, each so different with stonework like lace, ancient marble, graceful columns. . .the water of the canal washing over their green steps.'

'You've been here before?'

'Once, as a student. I stayed at the cheapest rooms near the church of Santo Stefano and gorged myself on museums and priceless works of art till I got artistic indigestion.'

Kirstie could hear the bells of the campaniles ringing eerily in the gloom. They were reaching the landing-stage near the Danieli Hotel, a Gothic palace that had been built for Doge Enrico Dandolo in the fourteenth century. Kirstie caught sight of a beautiful façade of elegant stone balconies, pillared windows and warm pink stonework.

They hurried across a balustraded bridge, guided by a porter from the hotel, Carson using his crutches to make agile leaps up and down. As the judge had been staying at the Danieli, they had taken him to a nearby hospice, a religious order run by nuns. It was a tall, crumbling building, the low timber door narrow and padlocked. They would have a job getting the stretcher out of that doorway, thought Kirstie, noting how Carson had to duck to go inside.

'Wait here, please,' said a little nun in Italian, swishing her long brown habit.

They were shown into a tiny, unfurnished cell. There was a small window high up in the wall. Kirstie was acutely aware of how much room the doctor occupied even when he was standing still. He leaned on his crutches, caught hold of her arm and pulled her against him in a mock show of affection.

'How would you like to be locked in a cell all night with me?' he asked, making her spine tingle at his closeness.

'I don't think that's quite what the Mother Superior has in mind,' she murmured stiffly.

'And there I've been lighting candles all week,' he teased, letting her go.

'Obviously the wrong candles,' said Kirstie. 'And perhaps at both ends. Hardly sensible, Doctor.'

Dr Black made a quick assessment of their patient. Judge Murray was badly injured though in a stable condition. The nuns had done all they could in the circumstances, and Dr Black was full of praise for their administrations. He had a smattering of Italian and was able to converse with the nuns. Luckily, Dr Cesaretti, a local doctor, knew some English, so between them they obtained enough information.

They moved their patient on to a vacuum mattress, then on to a scoop stretcher, which was the only way the judge could be transported. Kirstie plugged in a Laerdal sucker to take out the air and the mattress moulded itself round his body, making a firm support. She folded over blankets to keep him warm.

'Let's get going,' said Carson. 'This isn't going to be easy.'

It took several minutes to negotiate the awkward doorway with the help of the hotel porter and Dr Cesaretti. Kirstie did not breathe easily till their patient was being lifted into the water taxi. A woman hovered anxiously on the landing-stage, a lonely figure in the swirling mist. She was wrapped in elegant furs.

'Can I come with him?' she asked huskily. 'I'm his wife.'

Carson Black took in her white face and held out his hand. 'Of course,' he said. 'Take a seat here beside Sister Duvall.'

The judge was barely conscious but breathing fairly evenly, his face pale in the eerie yellow light. Kirstie checked the syringe pump on the saline drip attached to his arm. He was a man in his late fifties with greying hair and moustache, a strong aquiline nose. Hardly the sort of person prone to falling into canals among the bobbing gondolas.

It was cold near the water and Kirstie was glad of the parka that Carson Black had lent her. She made their patient as comfortable as possible in the confined space of the water taxi. He was well supported by the vacuum mattress and scoop. The sound of motorboats and forlorn ships' sirens were Venice, awash somewhere behind the fog, or perhaps the domes and palaces had already disappeared beneath the water of the lagoon.

The tall doctor delayed further assessment to a minimum till they were safely aboard the HS-125. He was ice-cool, almost detached in his examination, quite the most laconic doctor Kirstie had encountered, but there was no doubt he was thorough.

'There are internal injuries, but none that are hindering his breathing, probably fractured ribs, but they've not pierced the pleura and wounded the lung,' he told Kirstie. 'We should set up a blood transfusion now. Watch that saline drip doesn't run out and drag in air. It's getting low.' He checked the notes that the nuns had given him. 'Judge Murray is Group AB. I'll

give him another morphine injection in half an hour.
Perhaps you could have a word with his wife—she
looks pretty shocked.'

Kirstie rushed around. He had given her five different things to do all at once. She prepared the apparatus
for the transfusion, tucked a blanket round the judge's
wife and gave her hot tea to drink. She was a beautiful
woman with dark, raven hair smoothed away from an
ivory forehead, but pale and clammy. Her hand was
shaking as she took the tea, but she smiled her thanks.

'Try to rest,' said Kirstie. 'He's going to be all right.'

'I fish him out, you know,' the woman said, with a
slight mid-European accent. 'I don't know where I find
strength. He would have slipped under and drown.'

'But he didn't,' said Kirstie gently. 'You managed
to get him out, and he's quite safe.'

'We were returning from a diplomatic party in a
magnificent *palazzo*. It was foggy, but Edward wanted
to walk. He wouldn't take a water taxi. It was a lovely
waterside walk, like another world. I could believe we
were in another world. Then Edward slipped on some
wet stone and suddenly a vaporetto came out of the
fog—the next minute. . .'

Kirstie let her talk for a while. It would help to get
the trauma out of her system. As soon as she could,
Kirstie returned to assist the doctor with the transfusion. She hardly noticed the flight time passing.

'What's giving me this feeling that I'm being watched
like a hawk?' he said as Kirstie handed him the
aneurysm needle. 'What is it? Don't you trust my
technique? Kindly move, you're in my field of vision.
Are you expecting me to make some ghastly elemen-
tary mistake?'

Kirstie restrained herself from being too blunt, but

it was true. She had been unconsciously checking all his procedures.

'I'm sorry—it's just that I don't really know you. Any new doctor is an unknown quantity. I get a lot of new faces on missions. Many of our doctors are locums on call.'

'And you particularly don't trust a doctor who has the temerity to buy a business? You believe medicine and commerce shouldn't mix,' he added in a detached manner.

'You must admit it's strange. I've no idea whether you're a practising doctor or simply a career medic who collects directorships as well as letters after his name.'

He found a good vein in the judge's arm into which to introduce the intravenous cannula. 'You can put your mind at rest. I've been to medical school, qualified; worked in hospitals in major cities in England, spent two years as a consultant anaesthetist at a prestige hospital in the Middle East. Then last year everything got depressingly similar. I had a growing feeling of being imprisoned by my career—a sort of mid-life crisis,' he added with a wry grin. 'I knew I had to get out and do something different before I went crazy.'

Kirstie handed him some strapping. 'Is that why you were walking in India?' she asked.

'Yes, I needed space, time to think. I may go back to full-time medicine one day, I don't know. Now, having dissected me, do you feel better about having me around?'

'Yes, Doctor.'

'You can call me Carson except when professional propriety demands a more formal form of address.'

'Carson,' said Kirstie, her tongue tripping over the

unusual Christian name. It did not seem right. He was her boss.

She was as transparent as glass, and Carson could not resist a chuckle at her dilemma. There was something about her, a sort of innocent freshness that made him feel protective. Yet she was uncompromisingly honest with him, an approach which he was not used to.

'AAMS is lucky to have such a diligent sister on its staff, checking out the medics. I hope you won't be tempted back to the glamorous life of flitting around as an air hostess.'

He had intended to sound frivolous and she did not care for the patronising tone. Judge Murray was dozing, but she always wondered how much a patient could hear and understand.

'Never,' she said quietly. She wiped some moisture from the judge's forehead and spoke close to his ear.

'You're in the best possible hands, Judge Murray. You'll soon be home.' She thought she saw a flutter of his lashes, but she could not be sure.

'So what made you leave?' Carson would not drop the subject.

'I discovered I wanted to help people in a more positive way. We had first aid as part of our training, but it wasn't enough, not enough for me. I needed to know more. . . I had to know more.' Kirstie hesitated. She was not ready to tell him everything even when he was being pleasant to her. 'There were times when I couldn't cope. . .'

'Really? I can't imagine you not coping.'

'And I particularly like the air ambulance service because it's so immediate. Sometimes I'm giving the first proper nursing care to a patient after a traumatic accident. I can do a lot to reassure them. It's an important part of their recovery.'

She saw a shadow of strain darken his eyes to indigo. He had been standing a long time, and the cabin was a cramped place for a tall man. 'By the way, why don't you sit down while you've got the chance?' she added. 'You shouldn't be standing on that plaster more than you have to.'

'Yes, Sister, anything you say, Sister,' he said with irreverent obedience, but sat down with undisguised relief. 'You're right, as usual. Most disconcerting.'

'Are you coming on all the call-outs?'

'Whenever possible, if a doctor is necessary. That'll be one of the advantages of having a doctor for a boss. I hope you'll be able to think of others. . .'

There was a wicked flash of devilment in his eyes and Kirstie could have sworn he was thinking of those slow, butterfly kisses. Her own knees weakened just at the memory and an extraordinary pang pierced her heart. She had fallen for Sean's boyish charm in the same reckless way. It was for Sean she was grieving now, although she was beginning to think her pride was suffering the most.

'No doubt,' she said briskly. 'There are always times when I can do with an extra pair of hands.'

Later she returned to the judge's wife, alarmed to find her still shaking. She remembered what the woman had said about fishing her husband out of the water.

'Are you still in a damp dress?' Kirstie asked, moving the luxuriant furs aside. Mrs Murray was wearing an exquisite strapless dress in ruched floral chine satin. It had been soaked up to the waist, leaving a nasty tidemark from canal pollution. Kirstie pulled a curtain across quickly.

'Let's get you out of that,' she said.

It was while Kirstie was helping her out of the dress, towels and blankets ready to wrap round her, that she noticed the woman was finding it painful to move her arm. She winced.

'Can't you move your arm properly?' Kirstie asked. 'Does it hurt?'

'It's nothing, really.'

Kirstie went to the back of the plane where Carson was resting. 'I believe we have a second patient,' she said. 'A dislocated shoulder or worse. She can hardly move her arm. She must have injured it when she was pulling her husband out of the canal.'

'I'll have a look at it.'

He was amazingly gentle. The woman's shoulder was misshapen and very painful. 'You should have said that you were in pain,' he said. 'You must have this X-rayed to discover the extent of the damage. I think it's only a dislocation. Sister Duvall can make it more comfortable for you with a supporting sling and I'll give you some pain-killers to take.'

'You're very kind. . .'

Kirstie turned away from Carson, not wanting to be reminded of his sheer masculinity. His splendid six-foot-plus did not leave much room for her as she went to get a triangular bandage.

'You did well spotting that shoulder,' he told her. 'She never said a word. I suppose she was so shocked she didn't feel the pain until you started to move her arm.'

'Like footballers who go on playing despite injuries.'

'Something like that. Pain can be ignored in some circumstances. She obviously cares very much for her husband.'

Kirstie nodded slowly, sipping a quickly made

coffee. She knew about ignoring pain. 'A very fortunate couple, still very much in love.' She hesitated in case he threw scorn on her words, but he said nothing. 'Is he going to be all right?'

'I don't know. Despite the seriousness of his injuries, all the life signs are pretty stable. The pleura isn't punctured, although they may do a trephining operation on the skull if there's any pressure. He has a good chance of a full recovery.'

The plane made a silk-smooth landing, hardly a jolt at all. An ambulance was waiting on the tarmac as the small jet taxied over. The procedure for transferring their patient was smooth and efficient. In no time the judge would be at one of London's leading hospitals.

'Would you like to come with your husband?' Kirstie asked, turning to the woman who had been watching quietly during his careful removal. The seat was empty.

Kirstie glanced round the cabin and into the toilet. Mrs Murray was nowhere to be seen. She hurried over to Carson Black, a worried expression on her face.

'She's gone,' she said. 'I can't find her anywhere!'

Carson pointed to a figure walking across the tarmac in a different direction. It was the judge's wife, her fur coat swinging from her shoulders.

'Mrs Murray. . .and she's wearing my shirtwaister!' exclaimed Kirstie indignantly. 'Why ever has she rushed off like that?'

A stout woman in a tweed suit had arrived in a large official-looking car. She hurried over to the ambulance and looked intently at the man on the stretcher.

'Edward!' she scolded. 'I can't let you out of my sight for a minute!'

'Do you think she's the reason?' Carson asked. 'The

judge's wife? So much for your happily married love-birds. This looks more like the usual triangle.'

'Don't you believe in marriage?' Kirstie asked, wondering if she had imagined an edge of bitterness in his voice.

'No, I've seen too many go wrong. It causes too much unhappiness. Only blind fools get married.'

He swung away from her, not wanting to see the reaction in her expressive, dark-fringed hazel eyes. He had said it deliberately and harshly in order to warn her off, to make her aware of his resolution to remain totally heart-free.

'Very sensible in your case,' she said. 'I doubt if any woman could compete with your obsession for power. Owning AAMS is obviously number one in your priorities.'

# CHAPTER THREE

THE white sand of the endless Barbados beaches fringed the island like a pale collar of lace against the sea of sparkling blue. The sun glinted and danced on the waves in a dazzling display of shimmering light. Kirstie had managed to get some sleep on the long flight out and could now peer down at the island feeling alert and ready for whatever lay ahead. She watched the dark shadow that was their plane race over the waves below like a wide-winged insect seeking sanctuary at the Grantley Adams International Airport.

'I suppose you've been here before in your more glamorous role?' Carson asked, folding his arms and regarding her steadily.

'Many times,' she said, undismayed. She was getting used to his thinly veiled hostility. 'But we never stayed for long. The crew were normally put up at the Hilton, just outside Bridgetown, and we never had time for more than a sleep and a swim before taking another planeload back. We didn't see much of the island. I'd love to see the wild Atlantic east coast, all those great rollers.'

'Well, you won't get much chance this time either. Tantalising work. . .so near and yet so far.'

Kirstie was not sure if he was talking to himself or to her. She had begun to know the man a little better in the last few weeks, but he was still an enigma. She knew nothing about his past apart from what he had told her originally. Mid-life crisis indeed. . . She could not bring herself to believe it. There must have been more complex reasons.

Carson had accompanied her on several missions; other flights had used the services of a locum. She found herself looking out for his tall, lean figure hurrying across the tarmac with a medical bag, jacket flung over his shoulder, a clutch of papers in his hand ready to work on during the outward flight.

He was a workaholic. Often when she was going home, walking across to the car park, she could see the lights still burning in his office. Sometimes she saw his outline standing at a window, a coffee-cup in his hand. She wondered if he was throwing himself into work in order to forget some woman; she shook herself mentally at the absurdity. Dr Carson Black would have more sense than Sister Kirstie Duvall when it came to love.

Love. . . Was it love that she had felt for Sean? Despite her preoccupation with Sean, something had happened when Carson kissed her. Perhaps it was because she had been feeling particularly hurt and wounded. There had been a tenderness in those kisses which had gone straight to the hurt and sealed it into a silken cocoon.

'So it's another wind-surfing accident,' she said, dragging her mind back to the present. They were cruising in to a smooth landing.

'A woman wind-surfer and a speedboat collided. She's lucky that she hasn't lost her leg. There are facial injuries as well, but I'm not sure of the extent. She's at the Queen Elizabeth Hospital and creating trouble. A difficult patient, apparently. She may need plastic surgery at East Grinstead.'

'Poor woman, what an end to a holiday. Does she want to come home?'

'Definitely. The doctor says she's very distressed, blames the speedboat driver, a local lad. So lots of TLC, Sister.'

'Of course,' said Kirstie. 'Don't I always?'

But nothing was fated to go easily for the patient, a wealthy divorcee called Esmee Cartwright. They had only just landed when the pilot informed Carson Black that there was a malfunction in the undercarriage mechanism. They could not risk the long flight back to England with a faulty undercarriage.

'But how long will it take?' Carson asked impatiently.

'I can't say, Doctor. I'll have more idea after we've had a good look at it.'

A white hospital car took them the short distance to the hospital. Bridgetown was full of bustle, the narrow, dusty streets crowded with shoppers and strollers walking in the roadway, farmers wheeling carts of produce and leading animals, stray dogs chasing anything that moved. The new hospital had been built in lush green grounds, spilling with flowers and sweet-smelling shrubs.

Their patient was in a four-bedded ward, two walls of clear glass looking out on to the gardens. It was warm, but a fresh wind blew seawards, and everywhere was clean and bright. Mrs Cartwright's face was heavily bandaged, but her bloodshot eyes flashed with annoyance when she was told of the delay.

'This is unforgivable,' she said with some effort. 'I want to go home—I don't want to stay in this hospital. Can't you do something?'

Dr Black made an unhurried assessment of her condition, calming her with soothing comments.

'Your leg has been properly set in a full cast,' he told her. 'They've made a good job of it, and the internal bleeding has stopped.' He looked at the X-ray plates of her leg and skull. The break was high up in the femur, near the thigh. The facial injuries were whiplash injuries from the flailing tow-rope. 'The facial cuts should heal well. They might need a little tidying up, but we can't tell till those bandages come off. We could remove some of the bandages—they must be very hot.'

'I want to get out of here,' she insisted. 'I've had enough of this place. It's awful. . . I hate it! Please help me, Doctor. Please, Nurse?'

She turned imploring eyes on Kirstie, her voice becoming hysterical. Kirstie could understand the woman's distress. . .people often went to pieces in a foreign hospital, being nursed by strangers, no confidence in the treatment.

It was difficult to judge the woman's age or appearance, but, from her tanned skin and well-manicured hands, Kirstie reckoned she was in her late forties and took a lot of holidays.

'I'll stay with you,' said Kirstie. 'Perhaps I could wash your hair and make you feel more comfortable.'

'That's a good idea, Sister,' said Carson. 'Though I had been going to suggest supper at the Hilton in the Garden Room.'

Kirstie knew he was only being polite, but there was nothing she would have liked more than to have supper at the luxurious Hilton in the company of the handsome doctor. She knew they had got off to a bad start when they had first met, and, although their working relationship seemed to go well, they were icy cool on other occasions. The warmth of a Barbados evening might have melted a little of that ice.

'I'll take a raincheck on that invitation, Doctor,' she

said lightly. 'But I'd better stay here with Mrs Cartwright. Perhaps the hospital will give me some food.'

'The food's awful,' Mrs Cartwright grumbled. 'I can't eat anything. They just give me liquids.'

'With facial injuries that's the best nourishment for a few days. Think how much weight you'll be losing,' said Kirstie, making an inspired remark.

Carson took Kirstie aside. 'She'll let a Barbadian girl wait on table or make up her room at the hotel, but she has hysterics if one tries to nurse her.'

'It's lack of confidence in their ability,' said Kirstie. 'If she was here for a few more days, I'm sure she'd be won over by their kindness and care. They're excellent nurses.'

'There's nothing more I can do for the time being,' said Carson. 'I'm going back to the airport to check on that undercarriage repair. I'll be back in an hour. Don't run off with a handsome cricketer.'

'Depends on his batting average,' she replied.

Kirstie deliberately asked a soft-voiced Barbadian nurse to help her wash Mrs Cartwright's hair. They had to be extra careful about moving her, but the back of the bed let down and Kirstie was able to shampoo the highlighted curls in a basin, gently towelling the scalp afterwards.

'It'll dry in no time in this heat,' said Kirstie, making her comfortable again against the pillows.

'Well, that feels a lot better,' said Esmee Cartwright, sounding a lot less disgruntled. 'I could have scratched it to pieces.'

'It was full of blood and sand. How do you want it styled?'

'There's nothing wrong with my hands. I can do it myself. Would you pass me my handbag?'

Kirstie searched around the locker and the floor. 'Are you sure you've got it with you?'

'Pale brown leather, Gucci clasp. It must be here.'

'I can't see it.'

Esmee Cartwright was distraught when she realised that no one had picked up her bag from the beach and brought it along in the ambulance. 'And there's my jewels,' she sobbed. 'They're in the Sandy Lane Hotel safe. All my clothes, everything. . .'

Kirstie thought quickly. 'If you rest quietly and promise not to get upset, I'll go to the hotel and fetch your handbag and your jewellery,' she suggested, knowing she could be letting herself in for a lot of hassle. 'You'll have to let me have a letter of authority for the manager, and I'll have to check with Dr Black first.'

'Oh, Sister, will you do that for me? I'd be so grateful. And will you fetch some of my own clothes?' She plucked at the plain cotton hospital gown. 'This is horrid!'

Kirstie knew Bridgetown well with its noisy, colourful bustle of shops and market stalls; schooners and motor vessels loading and unloading goods in the Careenage, the inner harbour. But she would enjoy a drive along the fabulous west coast to St James's, where all the big hotels had been built. Sandy Lane was one of the most elite and luxurious, built by a British MP on an old sugar plantation in the 1930s, in the days when holidaying in Barbados was only for the super-rich and a package was something you sent in the post.

The cooling trade winds came in through the open windows, dispersing the heat of the afternoon. Esmee dozed, calmer now that she knew she would soon be going home. Kirstie leaned on the window-sill, enjoying the view and the sunshine, turning her face to the sun. She saw Carson arriving in a taxi, his jacket thrown over his shoulder, sleeves rolled up to the elbow. He looked up as if aware he was being watched.

Kirstie explained Mrs Cartwright's request to Carson as soon as he walked into the small ward, fully expecting him to say no.

'We'll both go,' he said, surprising her and taking her arm. 'The two of us will be twice as fast packing. We might even have time for a swim.'

'But what about Mrs Cartwright? We can't just leave her.'

'She's in perfectly capable hands. Her condition is stable and she'll sleep for hours. Apparently she was awake half the night demanding a private room. It'll be ten p.m. at least before we're ready to leave.'

Although it was late afternoon, the sun was still hot and Kirstie thought longingly of a swim. She was hardly breaking any rules when her own chief medical officer had suggested it.

'Give me five minutes to change,' she said, going into the staff washroom. She knew she could do it in five minutes. She tore off her stiff uniform and stood under a lukewarm shower to wash off the perspiration. In her bag she had a brief bikini in pale green that was neatly concealing. At the bottom of her bag, she saw the dress. She had been carrying round the chine satin rose-patterned dress since Venice, on the off chance that she might see the woman again. It had survived the canal water and dry-cleaning, living up to the reputation of its Paris label.

Sandy Lane was a supremely elegant hotel. Carson would pass anywhere with his rugged good looks, immaculate white trousers and tabbed white shirt.

Why should she have to turn up in a hot and crumpled uniform?

She slipped on the ruched satin dress and pulled up the zip. She had known that it would fit like a dream. It was a little too short, but that only showed off her long, shapely legs. She brushed out her silvery hair, fluffing out the sides, applied pink gloss to her lips and navy mascara to her lashes. Only the sensible sandals were wrong. . . She took them off and stuffed them in her bag. She would start a barefoot fashion.

Carson Black let out a long, slow breath when he caught sight of his chief nursing sister. She looked delectable, all pink and silvery, her bare shoulders smooth and creamy. Her glowing tiger's eyes challenged him to say anything complimentary. She was not in the market for masculine approval.

'Is this the new uniform?' he remarked.

'If it passes.'

'Cool, practical, morale-lifting. I should say it has a lot going for it. But haven't I seen it somewhere before?'

She should have known. His keen blue eyes missed nothing. She would have to tell him the truth.

'It's Mrs Murray's dress. . .well, not Mrs Murray, but remember Venice? The woman was soaking wet. I've had it dry-cleaned, hoping to give it back some day.'

Carson observed her confusion shrewdly. 'Don't feel guilty. As I recall, she walked off wearing your denim dress. A fair exchange.'

'Not in value. This probably cost eight or nine hundred pounds. Mine was forty pounds at a well-known chain store.'

He steered her out of the hospital, not commenting on the bare feet. It was all he could do to keep from touching those smooth shoulders or burying his face in that sweet-scented hair.

'Stop fussing. She'll get more wear out of your dress,' he said flatly.

A brightly coloured taxi was waiting outside, the dark-faced driver grinning. It set off with a great rattle of gears for the drive along the St James Platinum Coast road, giving Kirstie glimpses of the palm-lined sandy beaches, privately owned beach houses mingling with the wooden chattel houses of the local workers. The Barbadians sat outside their houses on the steps, playing music, eating, drinking, gossiping. Boys played cricket on the roadway until hooted out of the way by drivers.

'I can smell the sugar,' Kirstie breathed.

'Sugar-cane fields and sugar mills. The island's gold,' said Carson, smiling at her pleasure.

'Lynda Marshall wanted this trip,' said Kirstie, knowing Carson would hear all about it eventually. It had been an undignified argument, with the older woman determined to go to Barbados. It had taken all of Kirstie's tact and skill to point out that Lynda had done two missions without a break, and that a tired nurse was no good to anyone at all.

'What did you do?' asked Carson. 'Throw a dice?'

'Something like that. Loaded dice, she'll swear. She doesn't like it if I question her decisions.'

'Do you want me to say anything to her?'

'No, there's no need. I can handle it.'

Sandy Lane was a palatial eighteenth-century-style mansion set among mahogany trees and casuarinas, a beautiful setting for gracious living. A landscaped eighteen-hole golf course stretched inland. Through the distant trees, Kirstie caught sight of the sparkling emerald Caribbean. Her spirits soared. She was wearing exactly the right dress. The hotel guests were beginning to change into exotic outfits for the cocktail hour, drinks on the lawn or under a shady tree.

'Even the monkeys are taking up golf,' said Carson.

'Do they have to become members?'

'It's true. Sometimes the golf course is overrun with monkeys.'

Kirstie waited in the cool marble foyer while Carson introduced himself to the manager and presented his credentials. The staff could not have been more helpful.

'One of our beach boys found Mrs Cartwright's handbag and it is now in her room. If you would care to wait, Doctor, I need to make a few enquiries before I can allow you to take her jewel case. Of course, Sister Duvall may have the key to her room and pack whatever is necessary for Mrs Cartwright's flight home and stay in hospital.'

The manager's smile conveyed the impression that, if all nurses looked like Sister Duvall, he would willingly be ill any day.

'Perhaps we could have a swim while you make your enquiries,' Carson suggested. 'The sea looks very tempting.'

'With pleasure, Dr Black. The sea is free. Although the bay is reserved for hotel guests, anyone can swim from it if they walk up the coast. I will arrange for some towels.'

'How very kind. Thank you.'

Kirstie let herself into Esmee Cartwright's air-conditioned room. It was light and airy, with a refined elegance that was surprising for a tiny West Indian island. She took out a suitcase and began to fill it with silk undies and nightwear. She also put in clothes for

Mrs Cartwright's eventual departure from a London hospital. Everything was expensive and new. Kirstie also packed a smaller bag with an array of cosmetics from the glass-topped dressing-table and toiletries from the bathroom. She tried not to be envious of the display of wealth, for, despite all the luxurious possessions, the divorcee did not seem a very happy person.

'Finished?' asked Carson, meeting her at the door with two tall glasses, rimmed with iced sugar. 'How about a Rum Swizzle—a speciality of the bar, made with the best Barbados rum.'

'I'm on duty,' said Kirstie primly.

'I asked them to put in plenty of lime juice. We won't be flying for several hours yet.'

They walked down the wide, curving *Gone With the Wind*-style marble staircase out on to the pink-paved patio where guests danced nightly to a steel band. The gardens spread down to the sea, a riot of gaudy flowers and swaying palms.

'I suppose these are because you've got shares in the parent company or have a friend on the board?' said Kirstie, referring to the drinks.

'I should hate to disappoint you when you have me categorised down to the last share issue. What shall I confess to? Influence, old boys' network, or a handful of Barbadian dollars? I never travel without some local currency.'

The crescent-shaped beach was almost deserted, but the heat of the day still rose from the fine white sand. Music drifted across the waves from a red and black pirate schooner sailing back from a day's cruise. In the distance a group of fishermen were pulling in nets, singing an old song to regulate the work.

'This is so lovely,' said Kirstie, her bare feet sinking

into the warm sand. 'I can't believe this is called work. I'm feeling guilty.'

'Call it a tea break,' said Carson, wedging his glass into the sand. He began to strip off his shirt and trousers. His brown skin glistened in the slanting rays of the sun, shoulders rippling with muscles, legs long and lean. The plaster had been off a week now. He wore navy swimming briefs that emphasised his narrow hips. Kirstie concentrated on her drink. His body was far too attractive and she did not want to be caught looking at him.

Self-consciously she tugged at her zip, but in her haste it stuck. Carson turned her round, his fingers gently easing the teeth of the zip to mesh correctly.

'Slight technical hitch,' he said, taking the zip down slowly. The dress dropped over her slender hips and fell to the sand.

The bikini was suddenly far too small. Everything seemed exposed, her rounded breasts foaming out of the cups, her flat stomach quivering, the triangular pants barely concealing her neat, tight buttocks. A cool breeze came off the sea, and despite the heat she shivered involuntarily.

'Not cold, surely?'

'Just a ghost.'

'A seventeenth-century plantation worker, I expect. Did you catch a whiff of sugar?' His lean fingers caressed her bare skin, sending waves of sensation shuddering through her body. His hands slid over the curve of her shoulders, pulling her back against him. She could feel the tautness of his stomach and the dark hair on his chest brushing her spine.

'Please stop,' she whispered. 'This is. . .silly. We should keep a professional distance.'

'To hell with a professional distance,' he said

huskily. 'You look like a sea nymph, a pale green mermaid. I want to kiss you before you dive back into your cave beneath the sea. Once you've kissed a mermaid, then you're bewitched forever.'

'More likely to need a tetanus injection,' said Kirstie.

'My jabs are up to date.'

He turned her round to face him and she could see his blue eyes glinting with desire. Panic shot through her, and yet her need beckoned him with a traitorous limpness. She did not want to be kissed by him again. It was all too dangerous.

'No, please, Carson,' she went on, hurriedly. 'We're two adult, professional people, here to work. I'm not a casual kissing person. You caught me off guard once, but not again. I've shut up the shop and thrown away the key, so don't even try.'

'I'm intrigued,' he murmured, his mouth moving against her hair. 'Thrown away the key, eh? I shall have to do without.'

His dark head lowered, hair falling over his forehead in a fringe, his mouth touching the hollow of her throat. She froze as his warm breath moved over her skin, the tip of his tongue tasting the salt from her pores.

'No, the key's not here,' he said ridiculously. 'Nor here. Where have you hidden it, little mermaid?'

Kirstie gasped as his teeth gently nipped the tender lobe of her ear and his mouth traced the curve of her ear and the softness within. A hunger was growing that she had never known she possessed.

'I can't. . .stand. . .any more,' she breathed, a shiver of delight coursing through her as his mouth skimmed the sensitive skin of her eyelids. He was inspired. He kissed as no man kissed. She could believe that he was touched by some magic from the goddess of love. His masterful mouth made her dizzy with its sweetness.

'No need to stand,' he said swiftly. He lifted her off her feet, holding her close as they sank on to the warm sand. The hard length of his body covered her, the feel of skin meeting skin shattered the last of the alarm bells ringing in her head. She moved into a world that promised nothing but the wonder of his lovemaking. A small moan left her as she twined her arms round his strong neck and dug her fingers into his broad shoulders.

The waves lapped a soft song on the shore, the breeze rustled in the casuarina trees as at last his mouth found her lips and they both became lost in a kiss that filled them with wild, passionate longing. Their bodies trembled in anticipation of touching, feeling, every inch a discovery of joy. His hands were as ardent as his lips, finding the long, smooth length of her leg to stroke and caress.

She gave a low groan as his thumb sought the hard peak of her nipple and moved round it, pressing its delicious shape into the softness of her breast. She twisted and turned, trying to get away from the arousing pressure, but he followed her every movement, one long leg pinning her to the sand. His unyielding chest subdued her fighting, and as the last of her self-control ebbed away she longed to burrow closer into his arms, to become part of him, to be absorbed into his very skin.

'Like to buy pretty coral necklace for pretty lady, mister?'

A beach boy was grinning over them, dark eyes cheeky and impudent. His brown chest was bare, legs in multi-coloured beach shorts. He took advantage of

their shocked silence to go down on one knee and flick
open a smart leather briefcase. The lid of the case was
festooned with his wares, coral necklaces of all shades
and sizes.

Carson rolled over and groaned, shielding Kirstie
from the boy's gaze with his back.

'You picked a fine moment to start pitching a sale,'
he complained bitterly.

'I could see you really like pretty lady,' the young
vendor went on, unrepentant. 'See this one, very
special, match beautiful eyes.'

He held up a handful of vibrant green coral, tiny
and fragile. It moved as if it were still alive. The boy
was handsome and incorrigible, white teeth grinning,
hoping to make a last sale of the day before he went
off with his pals.

Carson pulled some notes from his trouser pockets.
'English money. How much?'

'Five pounds.'

'Two.'

'Three pounds.'

'Only because the lady is special,' said Carson,
counting out the money. 'Now I want you to go away.'

The boy transacted the sale quickly and snapped his
case shut with a cheerful laugh. 'Now I go!'

Carson fastened the necklace carefully round
Kirstie's slender neck, pushed back her shimmering
hair and gazed into the deep green of her eyes. He
sighed.

'Saved by a beach boy,' he teased, his eyes
narrowing.

She struggled to sit up, her hand flying to the cold
fragments of coral. 'Is this my payment?' she burst
out. 'Two pounds' worth?'

'I paid three,' he said.

'How dare you?' she snapped angrily. 'I suppose because you're my employer you think it gives you some sort of entertainment rights over me when we're delayed. Well, you're very much mistaken, Dr Black. It gives you no rights whatsoever!'

He was taken aback by her vehemence. 'You're mistaken, Kirstie. I wasn't asserting any rights. It was simply a normal male reaction on seeing a very beautiful woman in a very romantic situation.'

'You mean anybody would have done, provided they were willing?'

'I didn't say that,' he said harshly. 'Don't waste time on a postmortem, Sister. I can't guarantee another timely interruption. Let's swim. Unless, of course, you suffer from hydrophobia, extreme fear of water, as well as excessive guilt.'

He pulled her to her feet, a little roughly. His fingers adjusted her bikini bra which had gone somewhat astray during their close embrace. 'Tut, tut,' he added, brushing the revealed curves. 'Dishevelled again, Sister Duvall, and on duty.'

He dropped his hands abruptly and ran down the beach, diving cleanly into the sea. He came up yards further out, shaking his head, and began a powerful crawl towards an anchored yacht. Kirstie paddled into the water, dipping under her shoulders. It was blissfully clear and warm, and some of the tension began to ease from her. She could see shells on the sandy floor of the sea. She swam slowly, wondering if she was dreaming and would wake up to find herself dozing in the cramped cabin of the HS-125 on the flight back to chilly London.

But it was no dream. She could see Carson's dark head dipping into the water, coming up for breath, sparkling drops streaming from his thrashing arms. She was sorry for her outburst, but she had been frightened. The sun and the island were too seductive. She was afraid of Carson having power over her and she had been far too vulnerable in the tiny bikini, too much bare skin, too much opportunity. She dreaded any repeat of the Sean fiasco.

She turned and swam back to the shallows before Carson could see she had gone in. She stumbled up the sand, wrapped the big towel round her and wriggled out of the bikini. The flimsy, wet scraps of material dropped on to the sand. She planned to get into the dress before Carson came back, but, try as she could there was no way she was able to step into the dress or pull it over her head without letting go of the towel.

'So you didn't return to your cave,' he said, his good humour apparently returned. 'Allow me.'

He took the towel from her and held it out towards the sea as a shield. Only the fish could see her nakedness. She stepped into the dress and began struggling with the zip.

'Dear me,' he went on, 'you do need a lot of help with dressing and undressing.'

'Thank you,' she said, trying to sound dignified, as he zipped her up.

'No undies?' he mocked. 'Is this a deliberate policy to undermine my will-power?'

'They're in my bag in Mrs Cartwright's room.'

'Pity,' he sighed. 'The thought of travelling back with you only partly clothed would have been quite unnerving.'

With a slight nod, Kirstie left him to cope with changing by himself. She went to collect the luggage she had packed and found that the manager had the jewel case ready for them.

'Did you enjoy your swim, Sister?' he said, noting her wet hair.

'The sea is absolutely perfect,' she said, with one of her special smiles because she had side-stepped his question.

'Perhaps you will come and stay here one day?'

'Perhaps. . .one day. Even nurses can dream.'

Kirstie and Carson hardly exchanged a word on the drive back to the Queen Elizabeth Hospital. Kirstie was devastated that her body had let her down again; how could she have allowed all those sensuous kisses? She felt humiliated. Carson must be thinking she was a very easy conquest.

But there was no time for recriminations once they reached the hospital. Mrs Cartwright was awake and anxious to have her belongings. Carson phoned the airport to check on their new flight times.

'The hotel can put the rest of my things in store,' she said without a word of thanks. 'I shall probably return as soon as my leg is fit to stand on.'

Kirstie gritted her teeth. So much for all the hysterical pleading. She was about to comment when Carson returned, his face grave.

'We've a second passenger—a boy hit in the face by a cricket ball. He's conscious, but the sooner his eyes are checked, the better. He could lose his sight.'

The patient was in Casualty, a boy about the same age as the youthful beach vendor. The ball had hit him so hard that the seam had marked his skin, fracturing the cheekbone close to the optic nerve.

'There are three separate fractures of the cheekbone,' said Carson. 'They'll be left to heal naturally, but he'll be on a liquid diet for a couple of weeks.'

The boy was pale and shocked, a saline drip already attached to his arm. His face was badly swollen.

'Where are his parents?' Kirstie asked.

'You're going to have difficulty in believing this,' said Carson grimly. 'He's on holiday with a stepfather and a stepmother, one of those extended family situations. His natural mother was once married to the stepfather. Neither of the stepparents want to disrupt their holiday by returning to the UK with Mark. There are four other children to consider, some his, some hers. Mark doesn't know where his mother is. She's apparently gone on holiday with a new boyfriend.'

'That's awful! How the children suffer—all these broken marriages.'

'It's not for us to judge the circumstances,' said Carson. 'But we do have to do our best for Mark.'

Once aboard the aircraft, the boy was connected to an ECG monitor, and Kirstie took his temperature with a scanner on his forehead just before take-off. Gently she washed him and made him more comfortable in clean sheets and pyjamas.

'What's that?' he croaked.

'It's a scanner, a very clever strip of paper that records your temperature,' she said reassuringly. 'We can't use a mercury thermometer when we're flying.'

Carson checked Mark's vital signs, and the reaction of his pupils. The possibility of neurological problems could not be dismissed. If his temperature went up, they'd have to cool him down with ice. Kirstie took his temperature again at cruising altitude, then left the boy to rest.

But Mark's condition deteriorated during the flight. He was very sick and his facial injuries made it all the more distressing. Carson gave him an injection of hydroxyzine hydrochloride which sedated him with an antiemetic action. Once he had slipped off into drowsiness, Kirstie was able to clear up, freshen and ventilate the cabin. Mrs Cartwright had stopped complaining when she realised that Kirstie was rushed off her feet and that the boy needed a lot of her attention.

Kirstie was exhausted as the jet circled over Heathrow, waiting for permission to land. The scene on the beach had already receded to the back of her mind. What did a few kisses matter anyway? She could forget them.

Carson monitored Mark's vital signs again just before landing and after landing. They were crucial moments, and Carson breathed a sigh of relief as the plane taxied towards the waiting ambulances. He would go with the boy to hospital.

'I feel so sorry for that poor lad,' said Mrs Cartwright as they were transferring her to another ambulance. 'Nobody seems to care about him. I'll be out and about soon on crutches, won't I, Sister? I could hire a car with a driver and visit him in hospital, couldn't I?'

'That would be nice,' said Kirstie with a tired smile. 'He's going to a special eye hospital. I'll get the address for you.'

A long time later, as Kirstie finished her report and was ready to make her weary way home, she told Carson of Mrs Cartwright's offer.

'I hope she meant it. People often say things they don't mean. She could easily afford to go and see Mark—all that jewellery.'

'What jewellery?' Carson remarked. 'I didn't see anything special.'

'You looked in her jewel case? What a nerve! And how nosy.'

Carson slammed shut the door to his office. 'No need to look so indignant, Kirstie. I always check on unusual requests. We don't want to be caught smuggling any illegal goods—the odd rhino horn, for instance. But there was nothing to worry about in Mrs Cartwright's jewel case. All her jewellery was fake, just a lot of pretty glass.'

He left her abruptly. Moments later she heard the powerful sound of his car reversing out of the car park with far more acceleration than necessary, or so it seemed to her over-sensitive ears.

# CHAPTER FOUR

'DEAR Kirstie, why haven't you written? I'm getting worried about you! Thanks for the congratulations card, but I expected at least a letter from my sister, Sister! Tell that new boss of yours to stop working you so hard.'

Kirstie put down Kate's letter, unable to read on. Every word was brimming with happiness—all those exclamation marks. It sounded as if everything was going well for Kate's wedding plans.

'We've decided on turquoise for the bridesmaids— so don't wear turquoise!—with real flowers in their hair. The reception is going to be at Grasmere Hill Lodge, that lovely hotel with grounds that go down to the lake. You are coming, aren't you? We shall have to know soon, for the catering. Bring your latest—the more the merrier. I can't imagine myself a farmer's wife, all that feeding baby lambs in the kitchen, etc!'

Kirstie felt a momentary qualm for her sister. It sounded so naïve, as if Kate thought that being a farmer's wife was running barefoot through meadows and collecting apples in the orchard. Did she really know what it was like? Had she had a good look at the kind of hard life Sean would expect her to share?

Kirstie had been too confused and upset to write before. She had bought a huge, extravagant card and sent it off with a scribbled PS that her new boss was a tyrant. An unfair remark, she knew now. Carson Black drove himself the hardest.

They had taken on a full-time medical clerk, Millie,

to answer the phone in the office and contact staff, so the administration side was better organised. Lynda Marshall was appointed head of the nursing team and no one had an easy time. She was determined to make her authority felt.

She was a divorced woman, bringing up two sons on her own, and the strain showed in the deep furrows on her forehead. That she wore her dark hair pulled tightly back into a knot did not help to disguise the harsh map that life had drawn on her face.

'I see you were delayed in Barbados,' she said to Kirstie as she recorded details of the mission for the accounting procedure. 'You were lucky, as always. We had another rush job and I had to get a freelance in.'

Kirstie swallowed her indignation at the unfairness of the remark. 'Hardly my fault. I didn't arrange for the undercarriage to delay us. It could happen to anyone.'

'Are you arguing with me?' said Lynda sharply.

'No,' said Kirstie, wishing she had not spoken. 'Put me down for mud and floods. I'll pack my wellies.'

'There's no need to be flippant. I would remind you that I'm in charge of the nursing team now. Dr Black has given me full responsibility.'

And it's gone straight to your head, thought Kirstie. Lynda was acting like an old-style matron, all bustle and bristles. But she could hardly complain to Carson as he would only remind her that she had turned down the job. She knew he was disappointed that she had refused the position. To be truthful, she hardly understood her own motives, but the moment he had mentioned a company car her hackles had risen.

'No, thank you. My 1973 MG Midget will do me fine,' she bridled. 'It's cheap to run and fun to drive.'

'You can't be serious,' said Carson. 'It makes a

noise like a tractor. You need a new exhaust and a new engine.'

'I'll wait until I break down.'

'Not in my time, I hope,' he growled. 'So have it checked over now—and that's an order. Please think carefully about my offer. I know you'd make a very good team leader. You have all the right qualities.'

'I have thought it over, and I'd prefer not to accept your offer, sir,' she said, avoiding the steely glance in his eyes. 'If you'll excuse me, I have to list a new delivery of bandages. There are so many types now, thin gauze, gauze, support, elasticated, sticky—the choice is bewildering sometimes.'

'I'll leave you to cope with the stress of sorting bandages,' he said, striding off.

Kirstie watched his retreating back, stiff and unrelenting. She should have been flattered by his offer and she should not have responded so strongly. She wanted to work in an atmosphere of calmness so that everyone could concentrate. Instead she had created trouble. It must be the aftermath of Sean; she was not functioning on a stable axis yet.

Somehow she managed to catch up on her case notes and her sleep and tidy round her flat. She rented the attic floor of an old house in Richmond. Both rooms had low, sloping ceilings and dormer windows, and when the neighbouring trees were bare she could see the greeny grey of the River Thames, twisting and turning. She loved the river and could watch it for hours.

Her little flat was homely and comfortable, and she only wished she could spend more time in it. It seemed to be used mostly for sleeping and catching up on jet lag. Her house-warming party was two years overdue.

This was going to be her first weekend off in weeks.

She planned so many things, including a leisurely walk along the towpath with lunch in one of the many riverside pubs. . .an old film on the television, then a bath and bed early. It sounded idyllic. And somehow during the weekend she would make herself write a proper letter to Kate, though she was not sure what she could say. Kate was definitely in a matchmaking mood, so to mention the lack of an escort would be a mistake.

The telephone rang shrilly and for a moment Kirstie was tempted to grab her shopping basket and pretend she had not heard it. Surely not an emergency call out on her weekend off? Couldn't they find someone else?

'Kirstie?' She immediately recognised Carson's deep, gravelly voice.

'This is Kirstie Duvall,' she intoned. 'I'm sorry I'm not at home, but if you leave your name and number after the tone, I'll call you back.'

There was a pause as if Carson was waiting for the tone. As she did not own an answering machine, Kirstie was at a loss as to how to make the right sound.

'Hello? Kirstie? This is Carson Black. Sorry you're out. I wondered if you'd like to have dinner with me tonight? Short notice, I know. I'll call for you about six.'

He heard her surprised intake of breath and chuckled.

'Back already? That was a quick shopping trip.'

'I know it was a childish trick, but I thought it was Lynda ruining my weekend off.'

'Quite the reverse. I'm about to make your weekend memorable. I think it's time you and I had a little talk.'

'Have we got anything to talk about?' said Kirstie, immediately on the defensive.

'I should also like to make amends for certain boorish behaviour,' he said disarmingly. 'Can I tempt you with champagne and roses?'

'Not tempted.'

'You do eat, don't you? Sorry, I forgot. Raw seafood, isn't it?'

Kirstie could not stop herself laughing. 'Mermaids are a real pushover for a little lightly grilled plankton.'

'I know exactly the place. Please say you'll come. A simple meal together, nothing more, I promise.'

Something kindled inside her, a longing to be with someone kind and funny. She had been alone for a long time; that was why Sean's attentions had such a disastrous effect on her feelings. An evening of enthusiastic kisses and she had been smitten. It was ridiculous. She was old enough to know better, or perhaps no one was ever old enough.

'All right,' she said carefully. A simple meal could do no harm; it might even improve matters. A strained atmosphere was not conducive to good patient care. It would be sensible to iron out their differences and work harmoniously.

'Good. Come casual.'

'For champagne?' she put in quickly.

'I have to warn you that the butler has broken all the crystal glasses,' he said enigmatically, and rang off.

Kirstie hurried through her chores in double-quick time, cleaning, washing, shopping, watering her many plants. Then she wasted an hour trying to decide what to wear. Carson had not said where they were going. She did not want to dress for the Pizza Hut, only to find he had booked a table at the Ritz.

Her bedroom looked as if a cyclone had hit it. Suddenly she saw the time, raced into the bathroom, shampooed her hair under the shower, threw on pale

satin undies, sheer tights and then her favourite dress.
It was an ice-blue silk, several years old, straight and
sleek to the knees, then flaring out into a swirl of
shimmering material. Her short hair dried itself while
she applied her make-up with a swift and sure touch.
Silver drop earrings and a silver chain completed her
outfit, and she sure hoped it was somewhere special.
She gathered up a mohair stole as the bell rang.

Carson was leaning against the wall, arms folded, a
familiar pose that was utterly relaxed. For a second
she just looked at him, taking in the well-cut dark grey
suit, dazzling white striped shirt and silk tie, his unruly
hair tamed with a wet comb. Yes, it must be the Ritz.

He turned lazily, eyes sweeping over the slim blue
dress, the silvery-blonde hair fluffed round her delicate, heart-shaped face. His eyes darkened as if suddenly his thoughts were private.

'I should have known you lived by the river,' he
said.

'The mermaid syndrome. It was a long swim.'

'Your hair is still wet.'

'It's very quick for getting to Heathrow,' she said,
trying to make the conversation more normal. 'Along
Kew Road and then on to the M4. It only takes about
twenty minutes.' She knew she was babbling but she
could not stop herself.

'Twenty minutes if your car starts,' Carson insisted.
He took the key from her hand and locked the front
door as if she were a helpless child. 'Let me show you
a real car.'

She saw his car immediately. A ring of small boys
stood round it in an admiring throng. The shiny black
Lotus looked like something from a Bond film.

'A Lotus Esprit Turbo SE,' said Carson, like a
salesman. 'Powered by a turbo-charged, catalytic

exhaust converter, double overhead camshaft engine with four valves per cylinder.'

'But can it move?'

'It can reach nearly two point five times the legal limit. It rockets to sixty mph in four point seven seconds. And on unleaded petrol.'

'Eye-catching aerodynamics,' said Kirstie, impressed.

She stopped herself pointing out that few NHS doctors could afford such a vehicle. She tried to remind herself that it was none of her business.

Carson was standing round, talking to the other small boys, looking very pleased with himself.

'It is a beautiful car,' she admitted politely. 'I shall enjoy a drive in it, wherever we're going.'

'Up West,' he said, turning the car towards London.

It was a dream. The car was air-conditioned and the suspension was bliss. Kirstie sat back, determined to enjoy every minute.

'I didn't know we were near neighbours,' he remarked.

'Oh? Really?'

'I live at Strand-on-the-Green in an old fisherman's cottage. It's rather unusual because the building is raised in case of the high tides and flood waters. I love this area and, as you said, it's very convenient for Heathrow.'

Strand-on-the-Green was one of the most sought-after areas of the Thames, with delightful, picturesque riverside houses. Carson's fisherman's cottage must have cost a fortune.

Kirstie's heart contracted as yet more evidence of his money was forced down her throat.

'I love Richmond,' she said, looking deliberately out of the window. 'So many lovely seventeenth- and eighteenth-century houses, and the Old Deer Park. Did you know that Henry VII died at Richmond, and Elizabeth I, but there's nothing left of Richmond Palace, only a Tudor gateway on Richmond Green.'

'And Virginia and Leonard Woolf lived in Paradise Road, where they started the Hogarth Press.'

'I'm glad you take an interest in literature,' she said. 'I thought you were all profit and loss.'

'Only as far as AAMS is concerned.'

Carson drove well, with care and consideration, his powerful car forced to slow down in a build-up of traffic. She glanced sideways at him. The feeling of belonging at his side was achingly strong and she tried to dismiss it from her mind. His immaculate suit encouraged her to believe that her silky dress was just right. He slid back the sun-roof to let in the cool evening air.

'Not too much for you?' he asked. 'We don't want you to arrive blown to pieces.'

Kirstie shook her head. 'It's fine. I like the wind.'

'Real wind, yes. Cornish, Welsh, Cumbrian, but surely not this fume-ridden London stuff?'

A pang shot through her. The green hills of Cumbria came instantly into view, and with them Sean's boyish good looks and the strong warmth of his arms round her. She saw him striding over his farmland, his fair hair blowing as he took his dogs to find the sheep. She saw her sister at his side, her sweet young face lifted adoringly towards him.

Carson was still talking and she had not heard a word. He had left the weather and was holding forth about the damage to the ozone layer.

'You're a Green person, then?' said Kirstie, trying to cover her lapse of concentration.

'We're all going to be soon,' he said, turning into

the traffic slowly lumbering round Trafalgar Square. It
was crowded with tourists feeding the swarms of
pigeons, sitting on the fountain walls or paddling in
the basins.

'Hasn't changed much, has it?' said Carson. 'Once
Trafalgar Square was the site of the Royal Mews,
teeming with horses and stable-boys. Now it's teeming
with tourists and buses.'

'And pigeons.'

He grinned. 'The pigeons have squatters' rights.'

As he drove along the Strand, past the theatres and
shops, Kirstie felt a *frisson* of excitement. They were
heading for the Savoy or the Waldorf. She knew that
the Savoy's Riverside Room was one of the classiest
restaurants in town. She almost forgave him
everything.

He took a sudden right turn down towards the
Embankment and the back of Charing Cross Station,
nosing the car into a small side street, parking outside
a derelict shop front.

'We're here,' he said, switching off the engine and
closing the sun-roof. 'Get your things.'

He strode round to open the passenger door. Kirstie
got out, bemused. It was a shabby street with boarded-
up shop fronts, locked and barred warehouses, hardly
a lick of paint since Dickens's days. Carson took her
arm, almost jauntily, and led her down a narrow
courtyard called Carey's Yard, towards a dingy stone
archway and a door painted green.

He pushed open the door. They were in a bare stone
corridor. Kirstie was totally lost. Was he taking her to
some low-life but fashionable cellar eating place that
served exquisite Nouvelle Cuisine in the plainest of
surroundings?

'Not quite the Savoy,' he said, pushing open a pair of swing doors. 'But we get all their left-overs.'

They went into a long narrow room with high windows, lit harshly by fluorescent lights. Along one side was a formica-topped serving counter housing a tea urn, steaming aluminium containers of baked beans and sausages, a covered display of fruit cake and bread and butter. The rest of the room was taken up with assorted wooden tables and chairs, while at the far end a big television set flickered in front of a group of armchairs.

'Hello, Doc.' A toothy old woman sidled up to Carson, her weathered face grinning. 'Come in for a cuppa?'

'That's right, Mabel,' said Carson. 'The best cup of tea in town. How's your indigestion?'

'That stuff you gave me worked a treat,' she laughed hoarsely. Her rheumy eyes flickered over Kirstie, not missing a thing of her sleek appearance. 'This your lady friend, eh?'

'Alas, no,' said Carson, sounding genuinely regretful. 'This is Sister Duvall, one of my nurses.'

'You'd better snap 'er up before someone else does, Doc,' said Mabel with another gruff laugh.

'Hello there, Doc!'

'Evening, Doc. Nice to see yer.'

Carson acknowledged all the greetings with affable remarks and various enquiries which showed that he knew these people's troubles. Kirstie's disappointment and annoyance faded away very quickly in the face of what she was seeing. She took off her silver earrings and necklace and put them quietly in her handbag.

'The food smells good,' she said valiantly.

'It is good,' he said, leading her towards the kitchen area. 'Come and meet everyone. We serve only the best. For most of these people, it's the only decent meal they get in a day.'

The kitchen was hot and steaming, equipped with cookers and sinks, two young women in overalls rushing about in the confined space trying to do six things at once. They smiled and waved and nodded their hellos.

'Can't stop, Carson,' said a cheerful, freckle faced girl. 'Short-handed tonight. Two helpers haven't turned up.'

'And this is my surgery,' he said, taking Kirstie towards a white door. He unlocked it with a key from his key chain. It was another small room but fully equipped with an examination couch, oxygen equipment, drugs cabinet, as well as the usual desk, chair, washbasin.

Kirstie was beginning to get a glimmer of realisation. The quiet pride in Carson's face was obvious. He took some mail from the desk and began opening it.

'You work here?' she queried.

'When I've time. I do three clinics a week, mostly evenings. I try to keep to the same evenings so my patients know when to turn up. AAMS comes first, of course, but some of these people would never go to a regular doctor or a hospital. If I've a call-out, then I try to arrange for a locum to take my place.'

'And who pays for all this?' she asked, but she had already guessed the answer.

'Thornhill Drug Company. One of those money-grabbing businesses that you dislike so much, who make profit out of illness and disease. Everything at Carey's Yard is free—food, medicine, heat, somewhere to sit and talk. It's just unfortunate that we have to turn everyone out at ten p.m. Most of my helpers are volunteers with day jobs, and it would be unfair to make them stay any later.'

The cafeteria was filling up with a long line of homeless street people waiting to be served, their faces, both young and old, reflecting the hopelessness of their situation. Many were teenagers who had run away from home to find jobs in the big city, only to discover there was nothing for anyone without an address. They were poorly clothed, faces a bad colour, clutching plastic bags, shuffling in line.

To Carson they were simply humans that he could help, with either food, medicine or advice. The compassion on his dark, pirate's face was neither forced nor patronising. He was talking to many of them by name, asking after ailments, discussing problems and plans.

'I apologise if I've made insensitive remarks about Thornhill,' said Kirstie quietly. 'This is doing a good job. But I still don't approve of company cars, and in particular that flashy Lotus parked outside at a discreet distance.'

'Not guilty, Kirstie. The Lotus is my personal car, paid for by my Middle East stint, as is my house at Strand-on-the-Green. Overseas jobs are well paid. You are the only person I've offered assisted transport to because you're valuable and I can't afford to have my best nurse breaking down regularly on the M4.'

Kirstie coloured as the compliment fell sweetly on her ears. She remembered all the critical things she had said to him. She had misjudged him badly. Not many career doctors gave their free time to the care of the most helpless and unattractive section of the population.

'I've only broken down twice in the last month,' she said humbly.

The noise and clatter of the cafeteria was not unlike
that of a big hospital kitchen. Despite the plainness of
the surroundings, everywhere was clean and there
were bright pictures on the walls. The straggling queue
was growing and the young student serving was becoming more red-faced and harassed.

'Now you've seen Doc's Kitchen, we can go. I'll just
say cheerio,' said Carson.

Kirstie put her hand on his sleeve. It was an impul-
sive gesture, but already this was no ordinary evening.
It suddenly seemed very right that they should be here
together like this.

'We can't go,' she said, seeing her champagne
supper floating down the river. 'They're two helpers
short and here we are. Do you know how to serve
tea?'

'My best bedside trick,' he said, shrugging off his
jacket. 'But what about your pretty dress?'

'They've surely got another apron,' said Kirstie
briskly, all nurse, marching into the kitchen. In
moments she was swathed in an outsize apron and
Carson had a tea-towel slung round his waist. Kirstie
began serving sausages on toast, beans on toast, freshly
made scrambled eggs on toast, toast on toast. There
was rice pudding and jam for afters, or fruit cake.

'I like your new helper, Doc,' said an old fellow,
wearing several tweed overcoats despite the warmth of
the room. 'Wot a smasher!'

Carson looked across at Kirstie as she came through
with a fresh batch of toast. He nodded, cementing
something in her heart. 'Wot a smasher!' he agreed
with a wink.

Halfway through the evening Kirstie took off her
high heels. Her feet were really hurting. She smiled to
herself. So much for her champagne supper and fussing

about what to wear! Come casual, he had said, and now she knew. why. He had probably known all along that the cafeteria was short-handed and that she would volunteer to help.

By ten o'clock people began drifting away to cardboard city, the luckier ones to a hostel for the night. The kitchen was quickly cleared and cleaned, ready for the next day.

'Tired?' Carson asked as Kirstie untied the apron strings and hung it up behind a door.

'Exhausted,' she said, pushing her hair from a shiny face. 'And I thought ambulance work was hard! I never want to see another sausage again.'

She was tired and hungry. Lunch had been an apple a long time ago. It was too late to eat anywhere now, and besides, they were hot and untidy.

'Come and see London from the rooftop,' he said, picking up a covered basket. 'Then I'll drive you home.'

He had obviously forgotten about any food. Wearily she followed him up a bare stairway, across several landings. He took her hand for the last badly lit steps on to the roof.

Kirstie was past caring about any view, however spectacular, but it seemed quicker just to go where Carson took her. He pushed open a heavy steel fire door and helped her out on to a grey concrete flat roof.

'London. . .' he said, the warm timbre of his voice touched with something undefinable.

London with its myriad street lights, acres of rooftops, church spires and high-rise office blocks lay before them; the glow of suburbia lit the far skyline with a brush of orange. Lights twinkled on the Thames and riverboat music drifted up and over the noise of the traffic.

They leaned on the ornate, old-fashioned stone parapet, the fresh wind blowing their hair and removing the cooking odours from their clothes.

'This is my well-kept secret,' Carson said. 'I often come up here. . .for a breath of fresh air.'

Kirstie caught sight of a table and two chairs set in a windproof corner of the roof. The table was laid with a pink cloth and on it was a candle flickering in a jam jar. On the floor stood an ice bucket.

'The food is simple but good,' he said, putting a bowl of velvety peaches on the table and two covered plates from the basket. He draped her mohair wrap round her shoulders and pulled out a chair. She sank down, trying not to laugh.

'I warn you,' she said, 'I'm absolutely ravenous. I shall eat everything in sight.'

'I'm sorry it's not quite the Ritz,' he said. 'And I promised you a rose.' From behind his back he produced a single pink rose which he placed in a glass of water. He switched on a tape of Barry Manilow. 'We could even dance.'

'I doubt if I could manage a single step,' said Kirstie, rubbing one foot against the other. 'So this is where you kept disappearing to during the evening. And I thought you were having an impromptu clinic in your surgery!'

The music was soft and melodic, the night air warm for June, and a man she really liked and admired was pouring her champagne. It was hardly real, but for once she did not question her feelings.

'So the butler didn't break all the glasses,' she said over the top of the pale, bubbling liquid.

'I hid the last two from him.'

'I'm almost too tired to appreciate the novelty of this supper,' said Kirstie. 'But I am hungry, and it's lovely up here, and since you're driving I shall probably drink most of this delicious champagne.'

'I'm sorry if you'd planned an early night. I need very little sleep. I tend to forget that other people need their eight hours.'

He took the covers off the plates. Scrambled egg was piled in the centre of each plate, decorated with triangles of toast, parsley and sliced tomato.

'The upstairs version of downstairs food,' Kirstie smiled.

'How does it feel to be dining out with an entrepreneur?' he teased, his blue eyes glinting in the candlelight.

'No expense spared, obviously,' she said with a mouthful of scrambled egg. 'A whole egg each!'

'Does it make any difference that I do some good with the profits I make?'

'Of course,' said Kirstie, not wanting to talk about it, not wanting to spoil the easy familiarity that was growing between them. The champagne had gone straight to her head via an empty stomach and she was feeling floaty, utterly happy and floaty. She remembered their interrupted passion on the beach and a languorous warmth was spreading through her body. She knew it was only the champagne making her feel soft and tender, but it was a lovely feeling. Carson's dark face was etched sharply in the flickering candlelight, every line and plane becoming absurdly special. She became intensely aware of him, every movement he made, every word he was speaking.

'The profits you make?' she queried, picking up on the phrase.

'Thornhill Drug Company. My father owns it. I'm

their chief medical director, with responsibility mainly for research. We've two very interesting programmes in progress, one on ME and the other in Paris investigating the cancer deaths at the Pasteur Clinic. Somehow I fit that in, too, between AAMS flights.'

Kirstie swallowed a lump of cold toast. She could feel it grating her throat as it stuck somewhere along her gullet. Part of her brain was still functioning with clarity. She had heard of Thornhill Drugs and the takeover fight. It had been a battle between the giants for possession of a small but successful company. The giants had found it unacceptable that a family-owned, research-orientated company should be beating them at their own game.

'Your father's company?' she queried.

'That's right. He began as a very ordinary research chemist, named the company after the house where we lived.'

'There was a take-over bid. . .?'

'This escalated into an unacceptable situation. It went before the Monopolies Commission and for the moment Thornhill is still surviving independently. It's all part and parcel of my mixed-up frustrations. I was getting caught up in a world that was nothing to do with medicine, yet I couldn't let the big boys just swallow us up. And I didn't fit into any take-over the way I was expected to. I was too rough round the edges to occupy the pigeon-hole that was being carved out for me.'

'So that's why you went walkabout in India?'

'I could see myself getting into a rut that would be progressively harder to get out of as the years went by. That's why I bought the controlling shares in AAMS, to get back to ward-level medicine without actually ditching my other responsibilities for a hospital appointment.'

Kirstie's head was spinning. All this talk of take-overs and shares; it was way above her. She didn't want to know. Carson was peeling her a peach with his fine surgeon's fingers, putting it on her side plate. A cold wind ruffled the candle flame and the light flickered into the inky darkness in crazy circles.

'Eat up, sleepyhead,' he said. 'Then I'll take you home. We needn't clear up—I've arranged for someone to do it.'

The drive back to Richmond was all part of the dream. Carson put on a cassette of lazy, late night music. Kirstie knew that in the morning she was going to see and disapprove of the stark reality of his lifestyle. But now she pushed her scruples aside, floating on the champagne, tired beyond words, images of Sean and Carson all mixed up in her mind. Beware, said an inner voice, this has all happened before. . .

But Carson did not make it more difficult. He took her straight home, escorted her to the door, then left her with a chaste kiss on her forehead. She felt happy that he had not touched her.

She might have been more disturbed if she had seen him outside, sitting at the wheel of his powerful Lotus, hitting the steering-wheel with his fist. He could guess what her reaction was going to be.

'Damn, damn, damn,' he groaned. 'Why did I have to tell her? She's going to hate me in the morning.'

# CHAPTER FIVE

KIRSTIE hardly had time to even think about Carson in the morning. The phone rang just as she submerged herself in a foaming apple blossom-scented bath. She swore Lynda had X-ray eyes and always rang at the most inconvenient moment. She scrambled out, clutching a towel, dripping foam all over the floor. At least it was a quick way of giving the floor a wash.

'Hello,' she said. 'Sister Duvall.'

'Can you get here straight away?' said Lynda.

Kirstie dried and dressed at speed. She had a horrible gut feeling about this one. A young couple in Torremolinos, holidaying or honeymooning—she was not sure which—had been larking about on the balcony of their high-rise concrete hotel, and the young man had fallen. It was a wonder he had not been killed outright, but somehow he had survived the fall with severe neurological injuries. There was no question of anyone but Carson Black taking charge of this mission. They would be lucky if they got this patient home alive.

Kirstie knew she would have a badly shocked passenger to comfort. Sometimes the relatives were harder work than the patient, who was usually sedated and resting. This young woman, probably hysterical, would require all her skill and care.

Carson was also quiet and taciturn. He nodded briefly to her and started work on a bulky file of papers. Last night was last night, decided Kirstie, her thoughts mixed up, and never the twain shall meet.

He had obviously wanted to make a point, and, having made it, he need only be professionally polite to her in public.

Yet she desperately wanted to say something. To tell him that Carey's Yard was wonderful and could she help? To thank him for supper among the stars, for being the perfect companion.

But as she looked across at his face, carved in granite, not a glimmer of a smile, she knew she could not approach him. He had withdrawn into an austere formality that matched the drone of the engines, the crackle of the radio from the flight deck, the drifts of cloud outside the cabin window. She wanted to run, but there was nowhere to run to. For once, she felt trapped.

Do something, she told herself, and fast. So she got up and made coffee in the tiny galley, spilling the plastic beakers as she handed them round.

'Thank you, Sister,' said Carson, not even looking up. 'A bit early for coffee.'

'I didn't have time for breakfast and the bathroom floor got washed in apple blossom foam,' she said.

'Could start a new trend,' he said crisply.

'Not with my apple blossom. It costs too much.'

Kirstie sat down, cupping her hands round the hot drink, trying not to think of the turmoil she was getting herself into. Sean had seen her as more fascinating and flirtatious than she really was, and the result had been heartache. Now she was trying to be a caring and responsible person, and if she was not careful, the result was going to be. . .heartache.

'I like the new uniform, Sister,' said Carson, again without looking up. 'It's the first time I've seen you in it. Lynda Marshall has made a good choice. It looks good.'

Kirstie swallowed a gulp of coffee, almost scalding her throat. Lynda Marshall, indeed! The whole design of the new uniform had been hers. Kirstie had spent hours with a firm of uniform manufacturers, pooling ideas, testing material for laundering and creasing, heat and cold, ease of movement. That was why it had all taken so long. Lynda would have just picked something out of the catalogue, but Kirstie had wanted to design a uniform that was really special.

'Thank you, sir,' she said stiffly. 'Glad you like it.'

She could hardly say that Lynda Marshall had had nothing to do with it. He'd put it down to sour grapes. Anyway, he was not listening and had gone back to his paperwork.

She stretched out her legs in the slim white trousers, knowing they looked good on her. She wore the sleeveless top in polyester-cotton mix as they were going to a hot climate, with the long-sleeved safari shirt as a jacket. The shirt had four tabbed pockets which were useful and one showed the insignia of AAMS and the badge of her rank. Carson did not know yet that each nurse had the same outfit in navy with an additional long-sleeved jersey and anorak for cold climates.

They descended through the clouds, the ground a racing blur as they landed at Malaga Airport. The terminal buildings were seething with passengers waiting for delayed flights. It was an appalling sight, people trying to sleep on chairs, curled up on the floor, children crying. The conveyor-belt transportation of holiday-makers had broken down.

She would not want to come here for a holiday, thought Kirstie, as they drove the nine miles along the fast road at the foot of the Sierra Mijas, alongside the magnificent bay. Yet not many miles inland was the beautiful Andalucian countryside with remote villages and bleached hilltop castles, Granada, the Alhambra.

'This is not the place for me,' she murmured as she glimpsed crowded beaches peppered with umbrellas, the rash of towering hotels on the hills, the older streets jammed with traffic. 'To think this was once a sleepy fishing village!'

'You're going to say it's the fault of the entrepreneurs, developing the land, building all these hotels. But they've brought a sunshine holiday within the reach of thousands of people who otherwise wouldn't have been able to afford it.'

Carson was sitting in the front of the hospital car as the driver flung the vehicle along the roads without much care or consideration for pedestrians.

'That's all very well,' said Kirstie, clutching the seat as they swerved round a bend. 'But my comments do have an element of truth. You, as usual, see things from both sides. I only know I couldn't stand the crowds.'

'If it's all you can afford, you stake your claim on a square metre of sand and be thankful that the sun is free.'

Chastened, Kirstie shut her mouth. She was never going to argue with Carson Black again. Hadn't she said that before?

It was a fairly modern hospital, but over-stretched and over-utilised. The green shutters were faded, blinds pulled down, the wards stifling, fans creaking in the heat, corridors frenetic with overworked staff hurrying and trying to cope. The casualty department was packed with people waiting for attention; several were British, with burnt knees and Marks & Spencers shorts. Sunstroke, upset tummies, bites from jellyfish, twisted ankles. . .all the bravado went from travellers

abroad when they were unwell. It wilted away in the
heat.

Kirstie wished she could stop and help all of them,
but instead she could only flash a smile of sympathy as
she hurried after Dr Black's tall figure striding along a
corridor. Her Spanish would be needed on this
mission, and as soon as they were introduced to the
white-coated Dr Carlos Fuenta he burst into a rapid
prognosis which Kirstie had trouble keeping up with.

'*Está gravemente herido*,' he said, shaking his head.

Kirstie took a deep breath. 'The young man was
brought in at one-thirty this morning, unconscious,
pulse rapid and weak, breathing rapid and shallow.
He's been vomiting. Normal procedures carried out.
He regained consciousness briefly, then lapsed again,
and his level of responsiveness seems to have fallen.
Dr Fuenta thinks the concussion has led to compression of the skull and the pressure of blood on the brain
is building up. There's been some bleeding from the
ear.'

'Not good. Let's have a look at him,' said Carson.

He was only a youth, eighteen or nineteen at the
most. He was lying with his head tilted to one side, a
sterile dressing fixed with a light bandage over the ear.
He was breathing noisily and his face looked flushed
and dry. He was attached to a drip, ECG monitor, and
a catheter was in place. Carson took his pulse. It was
slow, full and bounding, unusually strong. Carefully
Carson raised the eyelids. As he thought, the pupils of
the eyes were different on either side, one pupil larger
than the other.

'What about paralysis?' he asked.

Kirstie translated. Dr Fuenta indicated weakness of
the right side.

'He needs a CAT scan immediately,' said Carson.

'Can they do that here? The blood is building up inside the skull. I'll give him a diuretic to reduce the pressure.'

'Is he well enough to be moved?' Kirstie asked.

Carson brooded on the question, his eyes darkening to navy. She ached for him, and the decisions he had to make. Her concern hovered in the air, unperceived like sound waves.

'The boy is desperately ill and he ought not to be moved for twenty-four hours. He could die without a Burr Hole operation,' Carson said. 'But his chances of recovery are far better in Britain than in this over-crowded place.' The boy had been screened off in a bustling ward and already two nurses with trolleys had bumped into the end of his bed. The level of noise was high. Kirstie understood Carson's dilemma. I'll help, she said silently. Rely on me. I'm here. Together we can do it.

'We'll hope his condition stabilises and his uncon-sciousness doesn't become any deeper. It's not a long flight home. With a good head wind, we can be home in two hours. Have you spoken to the girlfriend yet? Find out if she wants to come with us and exactly what happened. If she can remember anything,' he added drily.

The girl was sitting in a plastic chair, looking dread-ful and gazing at nothing. She was sunburnt with dishevelled brown hair and still wearing the short disco dress she had put on so happily the night before. Kirstie reckoned she was about seventeen, a mere baby to be abroad on her own, even with a boyfriend. She was not wearing a ring.

'Did you speak to her on the phone earlier?' Kirstie asked.

'No, the hotel management contacted us in this case.

They held all the travel documents, including the insurance. Hotels usually like to get rid of badly injured guests as soon as possible—it's not good for business.'

Kirstie drew up another plastic chair, aware of its legs scraping on the bare linoleum. 'Hello,' she said, taking the girl's lifeless hand. 'I'm Sister Duvall from the Air Ambulance Service. Dr Black and I have come to take you and your boyfriend home.'

The girl turned glazed eyes towards Kirstie's voice. She did not seem to be focusing on anything. Her neck was covered in insect bites.

'Hello?' Kirstie tried again. 'What's your name? Tell me your name.'

The girl's lips moved. 'Sandra,' she mumbled.

Kirstie rubbed the girl's hand, trying to initiate some response with the friction. 'Can you tell me what happened, Sandra? Can you tell me how your boyfriend got hurt?'

'Johnny—oh, Johnny!' said the girl, closing her eyes.

Kirstie went over to Carson, who was leaning over the boy's bed, taking his blood pressure. 'Her name is Sandra. She's in shock and she's been drinking. And she's covered in mosquito bites. I don't think they've done anything for her. I've loosened her clothes without exactly taking them off, and raised her feet. Perhaps you'd like to talk to her while I try and find her a drink to mop up the alcohol.'

Carson muttered something under his breath. He had seen it so many times when the distress of a relative or friend was ignored.

The long morning dragged on, watching the boy and trying to get some response from Sandra. Finding any tea was hopeless. Kirstie toured the crowded hospital, not a soul stopping her or asking who she was. In a ward kitchen she discovered some fresh lemonade which she laced with sugar. She brought back a brimming jugful with three plastic beakers.

'Drink this, Sandra,' she said, holding the beaker to the girl's ruby lips. 'You need to drink plenty. It's lovely and fresh. You won't be much use to Johnny if we don't get you sobered up fairly quickly.'

Sandra spluttered but began to drink, drops running down her chin. Tears filled her eyes and rolled silently over her cheeks, smudging her black eye make-up. Kirstie dabbed at the tears with a paper tissue.

'That's it. Have a good cry,' she urged. 'We're going to take Johnny home soon, to a hospital near London where he'll get the treatment he needs. Are you coming with us, or do you want to stay on here with your friends?'

Sandra did not appear to have heard a word. Her hands were plucking nervously at the hem of her vivid pink mini.

'This is absolutely hopeless,' said Kirstie. 'I can't get any sense out of her. I'm beginning to think she fell off the balcony too.'

Sandra suddenly broke into a paroxysm of sobs, falling back into the chair, her hands covering her face.

Carson looked down at the girl and shook his head. 'If I had a daughter her age, I certainly wouldn't let her off on a drinking holiday on her own.'

'You couldn't stop her,' said Kirstie. 'Lots of girls of her age go on holiday with boyfriends.'

'I'd like a few words with her parents,' he said grimly.

'Perhaps she hasn't got any,' said Kirstie, forgetting all about not arguing with him. 'Or they don't get on, or talk to each other. You can't pronounce judgement like some demi-god just because you're a surgeon and——'

She stopped abruptly. She had gone over the top again just when she had vowed to be sensible and pleasant and respectful to her employer. If only she did not get so heated about issues, it would all be so much easier.

'Sorry,' she said, her hand to her throat. She picked up the girl's minuscule disco bag. 'I get carried away. What are we doing?'

'This demi-god has made an executive decision. We'll take the girl with us. In her present state of mind, she might well be the next casualty over a balcony. Johnny's condition is improving, the pupils equalising and the pressure resolving. And he's showing some reaction to pain. Not much, but enough.'

'We're taking him home, then?'

'Yes. We'll have to move fast.'

Kirstie took down the drip and attached a syringe pump for the journey. Carson set the timing of the drops per minute.

The porters helped load the boy on to a vacuum mattress and scoop stretcher. The Spanish staff were relieved to be getting rid of a difficult case and gaining a much-needed bed at the same time for their queue of sunstroke patients.

By the time the ambulance had reached Malaga, another hair-raising journey, the girl had still not spoken. She was slumped in a corner, but her pulse-rate had steadied and she looked better. The boy was still breathing noisily, but there was no deterioration in his condition.

Kirstie looked across at Carson. Why was she so critical of him when everything he did was for the good of his patients? There was some strange streak in her that could not seem to accept what he did, why he did it, how he used the money he earned. She sank back into a slough of despond, shutting out everything, giving herself up to the solace of being alone.

She handed the empty jug back to the driver of the ambulance with one of her smiles.

'*Muchas gracias*,' she said. '*Nos gusta la limonada*!'

The driver responded with a torrent of Spanish, his eyes flashing, white teeth gleaming.

'What's he saying?' Carson asked, looking abruptly over his shoulder.

'He's trying to make a date,' said Kirstie. 'He has a cousin called Miguel who makes the best paella in Torremolinos.'

'And I have an aunt in Scunthorpe who makes the best Yorkshire Pudding north of Watford. Tell him you're busy right now.'

'He's very handsome,' Kirstie reflected.

'Don't tell me that mermaids are susceptible to earth men. I wonder what the secret is. . .perhaps I should have brought you seaweed instead of a rose last night.'

It was as though he had touched her. She felt emotion flash through her skin in waves. For once she could think of nothing to say. She wanted to throw deference to the sky and move close to him, stroke his arm, put her hand trustingly into his. They had had no chance to talk all day, no time to themselves. There had always been people around and so much to do.

The moment passed and Carson was beside the patient, giving instructions for the tricky aero-medical transfer. The patient was well secured, but it meant lifting the stretcher to a relatively steep angle. The captain and first officer were both experienced and able to help, but it was Carson who took the weight on his back, supporting and lifting the scoop till it could be slid aboard.

Kirstie hurried forward to support the tubing and IV lines. It was a well-known fact that any loop that might be caught would be caught.

'*Adios*,' Kirstie waved goodbye to her admirer. 'And *gracias*.'

'Do we have your full attention now, Sister?' Carson remarked.

'Yes, Doctor,' she said demurely.

Malaga Airport was going through another busy period with planes taking off every few minutes. The pilot radioed for clearance and the aircraft was slotted into the first available space. Kirstie sat behind Sandra for the take-off, concerned for the girl's unresponsive state.

'It's not drugs,' said Carson, taking the third seat. 'I checked for signs while you were getting the lemonade. Not a needle prick anywhere. She may have been prescribed some antihistamine for those awful bites, and that mixed up with too much cheap sangria and shock has practically knocked her out.'

'I'll find something soothing for the bites.'

Once the plane had taken off, soaring steeply through a thin haze of cloud and levelling off at thirty thousand feet, Kirstie busied herself with finding calamine lotion and applying it to the girl's neck and shoulders. Carson was monitoring the young man regularly, checking the size of his pupils and watching for any change in his unconsciousness. He was responding now to skin pinching on his right side where there had been a temporary paralysis and loss of sensation.

'You're too tall for this job,' said Kirstie, handing

him some tea. Carson was kneading the small of his back with his knuckles to ease the strain.

'You're right, Sister. What do you suggest? I could get a few inches lopped off, or advertise for a midget.'

'I believe they're developing a hormone that shrinks the calcium in bones.'

'I don't like the sound of that at all. I'll stay with backache.'

Sandra accepted the tea with a slight stirring of interest. She drank it silently, occasionally sighing deeply, her eyes still glazed and unseeing. She never once looked towards the stretcher along the other side of the plane.

'Is he going to be all right?' she asked suddenly.

'We don't know yet,' said Kirstie. 'When he gets to hospital he'll have a CAT scan, that's a computerised axial tomography, a special kind of X-ray that can look at every section of his skull. Then the surgeons will know the extent of the damage and whether he'll need an operation. But he seems a strong, healthy young man and I'm sure he'll pull through.'

Kirstie sounded more confident and optimistic than she felt. There was no point in distressing the girl with the alternatives.

'We'd only been dancing,' said Sandra.

'Dancing? How lovely. Where did you go?' Kirstie hoped that the girl was going to open up at last. She had forms to fill in and she had to know the circumstances of the accident.

'A disco. It was really nice—smashing music and really nice people.'

'Who did you go with?'

'There was me and Johnny, and my friend Angie and her boyfriend Derrick. It was really smashing, great music.'

Once Sandra started talking, there was no stopping her. Kirstie heard what everyone was wearing, what the DJ looked like, what hits were played. Sandra had a mass of trivial information locked up in her head. The soothing sound of the plane cruising through the endless blue was loosening her tongue. She told Kirstie everything that happened, or almost everything.

Towards the end of the narrative, she became distressed and Carson had to decide whether an injection of diazepam was needed. But there was no telling the cocktail of medication and drinks already inside the girl. He let her cry it out.

'Try to get some sleep, Sandra,' he advised. 'We'll wake you when we're coming into Heathrow.'

He guided Kirstie to the tail of the plane where they could talk but where there was hardly room to stand. Kirstie found herself staring at his brown throat and the tiny cleft in his square chin. This man's attractiveness was of supreme indifference to her, she told herself sternly, staring at a shirt button instead. It didn't help much as she found her heart racing with a yearning to move closer to him. Then she noticed that the button was sewn on with a different coloured thread, and this minute detail of bachelor helplessness fuelled an unexpected tenderness.

'Let's hear what happened,' he said, steadying her as the plane rode a slight disturbance.

'The four of them went disco dancing. They were all having a great time, apparently.'

'Disco dancing? Enlighten me, Sister.'

'Don't pretend that you're ninety. You know perfectly well what it is.' She gave the briefest of demonstrations in the confined space, well aware of his eyes lighting up with amusement. 'It was hot, so they drank a lot. They took some wine back to their hotel rooms.

It's a wonder they didn't both fall off the balcony.
Sandra doesn't remember how much she drank.'

'What then?'

'For some reason that I can't quite fathom, Johnny
wanted to get into the next bedroom, but the door was
locked from the inside. So with the courage of several
jugs of sangria inside him, he decided the best way in
was to climb along the outside balconies. Sandra last
remembers seeing him balanced on the wall, reaching
out to step around the dividing partition.'

'What floor were they on?'

'Third.'

'Johnny was lucky he wasn't killed. I suppose he fell
relaxed and that saved him. He could have broken his
neck. How's the girl?'

'She's asleep.'

'Do you think I could have another demonstration
of this disco-type dancing? I'd like to learn how to do
it.'

'Hardly the time or place, Doctor.'

Kirstie gave him a little push and moved away. She
was too conscious of him for comfort. He was hard to
resist when he was teasing, those craggy features
relaxed and friendly. She returned to their patients.
The girl was asleep, head lolling forward. Kirstie found
a pillow and put her in a more comfortable position.

An ambulance was waiting on the tarmac and the
unconscious youth was swiftly lifted out of the plane.
It was a difficult transfer down the steps and needed
everyone's concentration and skill.

He moaned softly as he was being rushed along the
corridors of the big Middlesex Hospital towards the X-
ray department. Kirstie bent towards him, noticing the
flickering lashes and white-rimmed mouth.

'You're all right, Johnny,' she said, close to his ear.

'You've been hurt in a fall and now you're in hospital and going to have an X-ray.'

'Not. . .' he breathed.

'Not what, Johnny?'

'Not Johnny. . .' he murmured, so low she could hardly hear. 'I'm Derrick. . . Derrick.' He sighed and lapsed back into the dark void he now inhabited.

Kirstie watched the swing doors opening and the trolley being wheeled in. So he was Derrick, not Johnny. And he had been in the wrong bedroom, or was it Johnny who had been in the wrong room?

Later that evening, she slid thankfully between the cool sheets of her bed in the quietness of her tree-top flat, the street-level noise distant and vague. She thought about the four friends on holiday and the mess they had got themselves into, partying and drinking, and it reminded her of the New Year party. It was the first time she had thought of Sean for a whole day. That was progress indeed. The hurt was healing before it could become a permanent part of her life. Even the disturbing presence of Carson Black could not take that satisfaction away from her.

# CHAPTER SIX

'SNOW? At this time of the year?' Kirstie could not keep the surprise out of her voice.

Straight away she knew she should not have shown any reaction on hearing Lynda's instructions. The older woman's eyes snapped shut with annoyance. She thrust a folder into Kirstie's hands and almost pushed her out of the office.

'Are you querying the information, Kirstie?' she glared. 'I'm quite capable of relaying the correct instructions to my staff.' She emphasised the pronoun to remind Kirstie of her place. 'This is a skiing accident in Austria and as far as we know the patient has a back injury. The highest peaks do still have snow in June, particularly after a cold spring.'

'I'll take my wellies,' said Kirstie.

Lynda shot her a glance that was spiked with malice. 'You're getting too big for your boots, Sister,' she said, unaware of making a joke. 'Don't think your friendship with Dr Black has gone unnoticed. It won't keep you out of trouble. We've all seen you playing up to him. It doesn't go down well with the other staff, you know.'

For a second Kirstie's mind went a total blank. Surely Lynda was not implying that her behaviour was out of line? A few kisses that seemed quite unreal now, a simple supper of scrambled eggs. . .

'Playing up to him? That's the overstatement of the year! But, in any case, it's none of their business,' said Kirstie, smarting under the unfair accusation. Had she

99

been too friendly of late? It was true, she had begun to feel differently about Carson, more mellow in her criticism of him. She had learned a lot about the man in those hours at Carey's Yard. She wanted to work there too, but hesitated for just that reason. Her motives might be misinterpreted. It was not easy striking just the right balance in a professional relationship, especially with a man like Carson Black.

Let's get to Innsbruck first, thought Kirstie, then she would sort it out. She hoped the tall, laconic doctor was coming with her. If the skier had a broken back, then bringing him home would be a tricky business and Carson's calm assurance a definite asset.

She had expected another routine day of office duty when she parked her car that morning. Lynda had elected to go on the last few missions. One had been to fetch a Euro MP who had suffered a heart attack in Strasbourg; another a yachting accident off the Côte d'Azur; and yesterday Lynda had been to Naples on a scheduled flight to bring back a woman with a broken arm. Now Lynda had run out of steam, deciding that cold weather and slush was not of much interest. She allocated the mission to Kirstie as if doing her a favour.

'Good, it's you,' said Carson, slamming shut the door from his office. 'I'll be able to relax. Lynda is an excellent nurse, but she seems to think she's running a twenty-bed ward mid-flight. It's a wonder I didn't get TPR and my blood pressure taken every hour!'

Kirstie hid a smile. Lynda would be in her element fussing around, but in the jet's small cabin it could be overpowering.

'A matron scorned is a sister warned,' she murmured.

'Just keep serving your delicious coffee,' he went on, striding ahead and pretending he had not heard.

Kirstie had to hurry to keep up. 'I've noticed the new brand you've introduced, or was that Lynda's idea?'

Kirstie coloured slightly. 'I'm sure Lynda would have changed the brand if she'd thought of it.'

'How charitable! Still, she made a good job of the new uniform. I like the navy outfit. Very neat.'

Kirstie busied herself aboard the small jet and then buried her head in her manual on airborne care. It still rankled that Lynda had taken all the credit for the new uniform, but Kirstie had left it far too late to remedy the situation now. She should have spoken up at once.

Suddenly she became aware of Carson beside her, holding out a beaker of coffee. 'I've decided it's sexist to always expect the female staff to make the refreshments, even if we do have aboard a member who's specially trained in that area.'

For once there was no sarcasm in his voice. Kirstie was pleased. Had he, at last, got over his resentment that she had once been cabin staff? The emotion was like wine, warming and heady, dangerously disturbing.

'How kind,' she said. 'Mmm, good too. I'm sure you could get a job as a steward any day if you reach another mid-life crisis.'

Carson almost spilt his drink. 'Didn't you ever learn in training that nurses are supposed to be polite to senior staff? I thought that was something they drilled into student nurses.'

'Of course, Doctor. Once we land at Innsbruck, I shall defer to you in every possible way, never fear. I don't consider the flight out as being on duty.'

'That's reassuring, Kirstie. I often wonder what's going on behind those tiger-bright eyes of yours. Whatever it is, you certainly show your claws at times.'

'I hope I haven't inadvertently scratched you.'

He moved aside the curtain of her hair and peered

closely at the white scar on her cheekbone. 'And how did you get this scar? Who scratched you? Did you meet another tiger?'

She trembled, very slightly. 'Not quite. Better educated than a wild animal.'

'What happened?'

'Someone h-hit me. . .' she said in a low voice.

She felt, rather than saw, his jaw set into a determined line. 'How barbaric,' he said.

He got up and sat in the seat behind her, suddenly thrown off balance by the surge of anger he felt at her admission. He remembered observing the sad droop of her shoulders on that first flight from Agra. Had she been thinking of some man, then? A man who ill-treated her? He felt his heart thudding as a torrent of feeling swept through him. He was amazed at the depth of his hostility towards this unknown man. Kirstie was a mystery and a sweet torture to him at the same time. How could he comfort her when she did not even appear to like him?

'Are you swotting up on backs?' he said, lightening the atmosphere. 'Mr Apple will need a lot of care.'

'Is that his name? Mr Apple?'

'Maybe Lynda has got it wrong—she does occasionally. It depends whether she has the right glasses with her. Apparently it was a Mr Pear who contacted us from the emergency centre at Hochgurgl. It sounded like a hoax at first, but the insurance company confirmed that policies were taken out in these names.'

'I think I know who they are. It's Apple and Pairs. P A I R S,' Kirstie added, spelling the second name. 'And you can drop the Misters. They'd both be mortally offended.'

'I'm lost. . .'

'It's Apple and Pairs, a new pop group. Heavy rock. Surely you've heard of them?'

'Now you're really making me feel about ninety! I like a lot of music, but rarely know who's playing. Perhaps I need guidance,' he suggested.

'They're often in the charts and on Top of the Pops. But since I don't want to be deaf before I'm thirty, I usually turn the volume down.'

'So you've a show-biz VIP to nurse on this flight?'

'All my patients are VIPs,' Kirstie murmured, her attention now riveted on the magnificent spectacle of icy peaks below and tiny Alpine villages clustered in the valleys. She loved mountains; their grandeur gave her intense pleasure.

'There's Innsbruck,' said Carson, over her shoulder. 'See the River Inn, and those red roofs and green domes? That's the old baroque town, very picturesque and medieval. Pity we don't have time to look around.'

Kirstie marvelled at the sheer sides of the Northern Alps which rose like a wall of ice at the far perimeter of the city of Innsbruck. It made a natural fortress against all foes.

'I suppose you've been here many times,' she remarked, as the sleek white hospital car took them along the fast autobahn.

'Are you suggesting I ski with the jet set?' said Carson, coming straight to the point. 'No, I don't. I value my arms and legs too much. A doctor in plaster is virtually useless to his profession.'

'Of course, Doctor,' said Kirstie. 'I do agree— unless there's a small brown dog involved,' she added, reminding him of Rauza still doing time in the kennels and the weeks when Carson's foot was in plaster.

'That was different. I'll risk a few limbs for cats, dogs and children.'

'Not women?'

'They can usually look after themselves. In many ways they're more capable than men, intellectually and physically. They live longer, are healthier.'

It was the last thing she had expected Carson to say. He was not a man to waste his breath on compliments, or was it a warning not to expect special treatment from him? But she had never used her femininity for any purpose whatever, in any area of her working or private life.

'That may be true,' she said. 'Unfortunately the one thing most of us lack is sheer brute strength. A man is always physically stronger.'

They were sitting alongside the driver. He drove very fast, expertly eating up the kilometres. It was a new design of vehicle used a lot in the States, less cumbersome than a large ambulance. The back was fitted with one stretcher and an excellent range of resuscitation equipment. Kirstie would be travelling in the back on the return journey, much to her relief. Carson's hard thigh was packed against her leg and the musk of his aftershave reminded her too strongly of her moments of weakness.

She shivered. Great banks of clouds were driving across the sky. It was already feeling colder as the road climbed towards Solden, an international sports centre. She was glad she had packed a thermal vest and socks. She just had to find a place where she could put them on.

'Somewhere up there is our patient, Apple,' said Carson, indicating a vast expanse of shimmering virgin snow and ice. 'Gaislachkogel is where you can ski practically all year round. It has the highest cable car in Austria, taking skiers up to the Otztal Alps.'

'It's so beautiful,' said Kirstie, feasting her eyes on

the snowy slopes and towering peaks, the sun glinting on glaciers.

Soon they reached tiny Obergurgl, the highest village in Austria. The welcome notice informed them it was at six thousand, three hundred and twenty feet. Now the car turned on to the Timmelsjoch High Alpine road which took them, twisting and turning through magnificent mountain scenery, towards where their patient was waiting.

'It's going to be a difficult transfer,' said Kirstie, dreading the long return journey.

Carson touched her hand briefly. 'We'll manage.'

The vista of sparkling ski-slopes and chair-lifts was awesome, but there was no time to waste admiring the view. They hurried into the emergency station at the ski-school at Hochgurgl, gulping in the cold air and searching for sunglasses against the glare of the snow. They were expecting to find their patient waiting, but he was not there. Nor was Pairs.

'Then where the devil are they?' Carson demanded to know of the distraught male attendant. 'Don't tell me we've come to the wrong place!'

'It's the helicopter, sir. It has not arrived yet, so the injured skier is still on the slope. It was an unfortunate accident. There was a soft patch of snow and he hit a rock.'

'Most unfortunate,' said Carson impatiently. 'Can I speak to someone? Are you in radio communication with the rescue team?'

'Of course. Come through to the next room, please.'

Kirstie took the opportunity to pull on her thick socks. Hochgurgl was a pretty place in the crisp and dazzling sunshine, but a sharp layer of cold air swept down from the snow and ice. And out there on those slopes were these two young pop musicians, their lives and careers changed instantly by a rock being in the wrong place at the wrong time.

Carson returned, his face thunderous. 'The helicopter should be here any minute now. I'll go with it to fetch the patient. The other skier is there too.'

'I'll get ready——' Kirstie began.

'No, you're not coming. It's going to be dangerous enough, picking up the injured man from the slope, and you'll only get in the way. Stay here and treat yourself to a coffee and some cream cakes.' He passed her some twenty-schilling notes. 'You're far too thin.'

'I don't have a sweet tooth.'

'It's your skin that wants filling out, not your teeth.'

There was no mistaking the sound of the helicopter overhead, its rotor blades clattering as it hovered above the landing-pad. A rope-ladder was thrown down. Carson ducked and ran out, hair flattened by the blast of air, his anorak flapping. He clambered aboard with hardly time to tumble into the cabin before the craft rose again and the door slid shut.

The helicopter veered away in a sideways crab-like manoeuvre, then gained height and roared off towards Gaislachkogel. In moments it was just a black insect climbing the white mountain face.

Kirstie felt deserted and abandoned. She put on a cheerful face and exchanged a few reassuring words with the attendant. She decided to look around the delightful ski centre, enjoy the unexpected lull in her work, and find a cloakroom where she could slip on the thermal vest.

In a little rustic café she ordered hot frothy coffee in a tall glass and a mouth-watering cream cake sprinkled with cinnamon and nuts. She sat at a window table, absorbed in the view, alert for any sign or sound of the helicopter returning.

Kirstie knew it was going to be a nightmare unloading a back injury from such a high cabin door, all the dust and snow flying up, the landing-pad's hard-packed snow making a slippery surface. The helicopter's noise and vibrations were another disadvantage, but its ability to hover outweighed everything else in mountain-rescue work.

Suddenly she saw a black speck in the distance and she gulped down the last of her coffee, and pulled on her navy anorak before hurrying out of the café. The male attendant also appeared, relieved that something was happening at last. The helicopter came swooping towards them like a black dragon-fly, making a sudden abrupt reverse swing that gave every impression of it spinning out of control.

Kirstie froze, her heart thudding wildly, fear leaping to her throat. It was going to crash. She was going to witness a disaster. There was no sense of time, nothing moved in that moment of prolonged, suspended motion. The scene was a black and white still photograph, the monstrous machine darkly black against the backdrop of snow. She saw the tail dip and a pain of anguish splintered her mind. Her imagination saw the helicopter exploding into flames, debris and acrid smoke leaping into the air.

It was in that second of stunned horror that Kirstie realised that she loved Carson and he meant more to her than any human being in existence. The thought of losing him was shattering. It was as if someone had stabbed her in the heart, and she felt a sudden, constricting pain in her chest that made her gasp.

It only took that fleeting space of time to make her aware of the strength of her new feelings. Her heart began to race as the revelation shook her with sharp, poignant despair. She cried out his name silently.

Windmills in her head began to spin, her pulse pounding, the vibrations going down her body and into the very ground.

Then she realised that the helicopter had come out of its mad spin, steadied itself and drifted down on to the landing-pad. It was the vibration of its engines that she could feel through her feet, the rotor blades still turning slowly.

The door slid open and Carson leapt out, head down as he ran across to her.

'Come on, get in,' he shouted. 'We're going to Innsbruck. It'll save that long drive.'

'Carson. . .' she said weakly, unable to think straight from seeing him so tall, so vibrant, whole, unhurt. 'Are you all right?'

'What's the matter? You look white.'

'Carson—Carson.' She trembled. She could only repeat his name over and over again.

'Move, Kirstie. We haven't got all day.'

She shook her head, the wind racing past her ears as he dragged her across to the helicopter. How could she tell him? What was there to say? She was only just aware of these tender feelings, too fragile to put into words, too delicate to expose to daylight. At the same time, part of her was resisting the way she felt, outraged that she should be entering another situation where she could be hurt. Hadn't Sean been enough? She was only laying herself open to more and deeper humiliation. She refused to go through that kind of heartbreak again.

Kirstie felt as if she was being pulled through billows of air as Carson hustled her towards the open door. It yawned into darkness.

'I've never been in a helicopter,' she protested.

'Now's your chance. Hop in.'

Hop in! She glared at him, dismayed that he did not realise how frightened she had been, what she had just gone through, that he was unaware of how she was feeling. And now he wanted her to jump a ridiculous height. He was impossible!

Carson put his hands under her armpits in a punishing grip, swung her off the ground and heaved her bodily into the helicopter. She sprawled on to the floor in an ungainly position, thankful she was wearing trousers, furious at his manhandling.

'Dr Black!' she began.

'You're on duty now, Sister,' he reminded her sternly. 'Deference, politeness. . .remember?'

Kirstie swallowed her indignation in the relief of knowing he was safe and completely back to normal. She hugged that knowledge to herself possessively. He must never know how frightened she had been. He might find it irritating, and that would hurt. This was a love that would have to be hidden away forever. She must not betray her feelings with a single word, a single touch. It would be hard.

She allowed herself the briefest of moments to enjoy the novelty of the vertical lift-off. After years of flying jets, it was an exciting sensation, like being at a fairground. Now she understood the sideways veering before it turned and headed down the valley.

But there was no time to admire the snowy slopes. Kirstie put on ear-protectors and gave her full attention to their patient lying on the floor of the helicopter. She recognised the thin sharp features and crew-cut hair of the singer guitarist, Apple. His partner, the drummer Pairs, was crouched at the back of the helicopter, his head in his hands, clutching a woollen ski-hat.

Apple was already packed in a vacuum mattress

with a neck collar to restrict the amount of movement. It was cold in the helicopter, and Kirstie covered him with a thermal blanket from her medical kit to conserve his body heat. She rolled up a couple of towels and packed them round his head, taking care not to move the protectors lightly taped over his ears.

He opened his eyes. They were a pale blue, almost lost against the pallor of his skin, a very different blue from the doctor's eyes. There was none of Carson's depth or intensity of colour.

Kirstie gave him a warm smile. 'Hello,' she said. 'Don't worry, we're taking care of you.' He responded slightly, which was a good sign. He was not comatose. It meant he might not have any serious brain damage.

Carson Black and Kirstie worked instinctively together, without words. There was little chance of hearing each other over the noise of the rotor blades.

The flight was swift and direct to Innsbruck. The pilot set his powerful machine down as gently as a bird landing. Kirstie took off the ear-protectors and shook out her silvery hair.

'Thank goodness for that! Apart from the noise, what a marvellous trip.' She turned to thank the pilot in her usual polite way.

'Come along, Sister,' said Carson darkly. 'No wasting time. Let's get our patient transferred.'

'It doesn't take a second to thank anyone,' she said.

'Meaning I never thank you?'

'Meaning you can take it any way you like, sir,' she said with a sweet smile that took all the sting out of her words.

Once aboard the aircraft they were able to make the young musician more comfortable. First Kirstie removed his heavy ski-boots. He was shocked and in some pain. His hands and feet were numb and swollen.

'Can you feel anything?' Carson asked during the examination. 'Here? Here?'

'I've got a grotty headache.'

'I'll give you something for that and a steroid injection for the inflammation and swelling. The nerves will be blocked and we need to reduce the swelling before we can detect any potential damage.'

'I've some tingling in my fingers.'

'That's a good sign.'

Carson immediately set up a new drip with a syringe pump while Kirstie washed as much of the young man as possible without disturbing him. Carson had already given him an injection of morphine for the helicopter journey, so he was pretty sleepy. It was necessary to put him in some form of traction with skull-tongs, though impossible to use weights and pulleys because of the roll and pitch of the plane.

Kirstie set up the Rambaud cervical traction frame and attached it to the stretcher. This allowed the tension of the skull-tongs to be controlled and measured on a spring scale. She fitted more tightly rolled towels each side of his head and neck, paying close attention to any areas of body pressure which might go unnoticed due to his lack of feeling. Bladder function was controlled with a catheter.

The other half of the pop duo was watching the preparations with alarm, although he had recovered a certain chirpiness since boarding the familiar executive jet.

'What's that, Doc?' he asked. 'Looks like medieval torture.'

'Deceptive appearance. It's the best way of keeping a cervical spine injury in traction during a flight. Any movement could increase the crack in the vertebra.

Don't worry, it's not hurting your friend. In fact, it should help ease the pain.'

'What's he done? Broken his neck? Is he going to be all right?'

'I can't say without seeing a full set of X-rays.'

Carson took Kirstie aside. 'I should guess he has a fractured dislocation—C4 possibly—but there's a good chance that the spinal cord is only stretched, not severed.'

'Could they operate?'

'There's a procedure called decompression reduction with internal fixation. It's a difficult operation, but in the hands of a top neuro-surgeon can be very successful.'

'He's got to have the tops,' Pairs put in. 'My boy's special.'

Kirstie was full of sympathy for their patient. It was a serious operation with a difficult recovery period. He might be paralysed or have a partial paralysis. It might be the end of his performing career, but if it was a simple neck crack, it could mend with a complete recovery.

'It's a joke, you know,' said Pairs, scratching his equally short hair. 'We came here on the spin of a coin—heads Austria, tails Malta. And I reckon Apple used his two-headed coin because he wanted to learn to ski and chat up all the drones.'

'Drones?' queried Carson.

'Sloanes, mate. Them upper-class birds. Apple fancied a really upper-class girl, a smooth blonde from Eaton Square, Belgravia. Like your nurse here. She's neat. What a pair of pegs!'

'Tell him I live in an attic in Richmond,' Kirstie murmured.

Carson's eyebrows drew together in a dark frown of

concentration. 'I'm usually too busy to notice such things, but I do agree that Sister Duvall has a fine pair of pegs.'

Kirstie nearly dropped the tea she was making. She blamed it on slight turbulence. One minute Carson was annoyed with her, then the next making facetious remarks, all in that same laconic manner. She could hardly look at him, afraid that the tenderness in her eyes would give her away. She was not going to get caught a second time. No hopes, no expectations. . .this time she would keep the situation under control. No one would know and nothing would happen.

'Rosie Lee, mate?' she said, sliding up to Carson, letting him know she had heard the appreciation of her legs.

'Er. . .yes, thank you, Sister,' he managed to say, nonplussed for a second, then recovering.

It was only a two-hour flight back from Austria, but Kirstie had plenty to do monitoring the young musician. They were fifteen minutes from Gatwick, where Apple was being admitted to a private clinic, when Kirstie noticed the drummer having some difficulty in breathing. He was wheezing noisily, rasping in irregular gulps of air. She hurried over to him.

'Are you all right?' she asked. 'Are you asthmatic? Are you having an asthma attack?'

'Yes,' he said hoarsely, trying to get his breath.

'Where's your Ventilin inhaler?'

'Lost. . .it.'

The young man was showing early signs of oxygen starvation, his face tinged with blue. Kirstie knew they carried inhalers, but first leaned him forward with a pillow for support. She hurried for the oxygen equipment, and Carson, alerted by sounds of activity, came through from the flight deck. He immediately helped her with the bulky cylinder, adjusted the flow rate to six litres per minute while Kirstie held the simple mask over Pairs' nose and mouth. He gasped, drawing in the life-saving oxygen.

'And a two-hundred-mls hydrocortisone injection, please, Sister.'

Kirstie prepared the injection, swabbed Pairs' arm with antiseptic and let the doctor insert it into a vein, though this was a procedure she was quite capable of doing herself.

The fight for breath was always disturbing to watch, but gradually the cyanosed appearance lessened, his pulse-rate fell and his breathing became more relaxed. He removed the mask from his face and grinned weakly.

'Sorry, folks. Bloody nuisance, this asthma. And I can't. . .get the hang of that damned inhaler.'

'You should persevere,' said Kirstie. 'It could save your life. I'll show you how. I know they're not easy to use.'

'You can teach me anything, any time, Sister,' he grinned, but with a lot less of his normal cheekiness.

They transferred both patients to the smart private clinic outside Gatwick. A neuro-surgeon had already travelled down from London. He met Carson Black in the flower-filled, panelled reception area and they were soon deep in discussion. Kirstie was not too tired to appreciate the comfort and luxury of the place; it was like a hotel. No smell of disinfectant, no clattering trolleys.

She was becoming far too hot in her thermal vest and socks. The tedious journey home loomed ahead; Gatwick to Victoria on the train, underground out to Richmond, all the crowds and stoppages. It would be

at least two hours before she was home. And what
about the equipment still on the plane? She did not
want to get into trouble.

She waited in the quietness of the reception, half
dozing, wondering if Carson would travel back with
her or if he would go scooting off on another commitment. He might be staying on to observe the intricate
operation.

He appeared from the lift, carrying his anorak. For
once he looked tired, the strain showing around his
eyes and the tightness of his mouth.

'I've found us a lift home,' he said bluntly.

'Thank goodness! I couldn't cope with British Rail.'

She followed his tall figure out into the hospital car
park, the droop of his shoulders cementing the softness
of love she was feeling for him. She would love him in
her own special way. She allowed herself to imagine
taking him into her arms and soothing away that
tension with all the sweetness in her power.

Instead she said: 'Lynda's going to be mad.'

He looked down at her quizzically. 'Why?'

'Lynda's two boys are great fans of Apple and Pairs.
If she'd gone on this mission, she could have got their
autographs for her boys which would have made her
Mum of the Year.'

'I hardly think that Apple, as he calls himself, was
in a fit state to sign autographs.'

With a secret smile of triumph, Kirstie produced
two small cards from her pocket. 'Pairs gave me these
as a souvenir. Their chair-lift passes, both signed!'

Carson started to laugh. 'What price fame! Nobody
asks me to autograph their operations. So what are
you going to do with them? Get them framed?'

'Something far more inspired. I've just nominated
myself Friend of the Year,' said Kirstie, putting the

cards safely back in her pocket. 'I shall give them to Lynda while apologising humbly for not checking in the equipment.'

'How could you be so devious?' he said, teasing. 'Trying to get out of trouble with a bribe! Perhaps it's cerebral frost-bite. A mermaid with snow in her hair. It could be painful.'

Kirstie's hand went quickly to her hair, then she realised he was referring to its pale colour. He moved fractionally closer, and Kirstie stiffened. She did not want any repetition of those heady moments on the beach.

He felt her defensiveness, heard a brief despairing sigh, and stopped, equally disturbed. She seemed to be upset, not her usual composed self. He wondered if it was something he had said. She was always such an enigma. The fire in her eyes had faded and their colour was almost the dark green of a woodland pool. Her long lashes were fluttering with the emotional strain of the last few hours.

For a second Carson felt a yearning to take her in his arms, but it was a weakness he kept strictly in check. He valued his freedom, his independence, being heart-whole. He had seen what marriage and motherhood had done to his sister Grace. There was no way he was ever going to put himself through the same trauma.

'Don't say I never say thank you,' he said, dropping a light, friendly kiss on the top of her head. 'Come along, sleepyhead, our lift's waiting.'

# CHAPTER SEVEN

STRUGGLING to wake from her dream, Kirstie found herself overwhelmed with deep sobs of despair. She had been reliving the moment when the helicopter seemed doomed to crash and she realised how much she loved Carson.

She was clammy with sweat, the sheet tossed to the floor, and she was gripping the pillow as if it were a lifeline. Rumbles of thunder died away as a distant storm travelled through the sky. She opened her eyes, relieved that the horror was not true, and the proportions of her room came into view with easy familiarity. She turned on her bedside lamp and the room flooded with subdued light, outlining the pictures on the walls, the vase of fading flowers, the clothes shed the night before in haste. Vaguely she heard a telephone ringing, but its purport did not register at first. She put out a hand to find the receiver.

'Kirstie? Wake up, girl. We've got a mission to the Middle East. You'll like this one—it's a premature baby to bring back to Great Ormond Street.'

'Carson, do you know what time it is?'

'It's half an hour past when I should have phoned you. I let you get some extra sleep.'

'Doesn't Lynda want to go? All that sand and sunshine,' Kirstie yawned. 'Right up her street.'

'No, on two counts,' said Carson, sounding a trifle impatient. 'She hasn't done midwifery for years, and secondly, she has a cold. You can't nurse a prem with

117

a cold. Can you be here in twenty minutes? I've already got a plane standing by.'

'Twenty minutes and I'd break my neck.'

'Twenty-five, then. Your neck is too precious. And if your car won't start, for heaven's sake get a taxi.'

It was going to be hot, she thought as she rolled off the bed. She had been many times to the Middle East, ferrying pilgrims to Mecca. A lot of the pilgrims had been women, their faces covered in batula masks, women who had never flown before and were terrified. One small baby to look after would be simple compared to a planeload of purple-stained women who would not remove their leather masks even to be sick.

'Where are we going?' Kirstie asked as she struggled out of her short cotton nightie and stood naked on the floor, stretching her arms above her head. It was just as well he could not see her.

'The Gulf of Oman.'

'I'm on my way.'

She showered in thirty seconds, threw on a baggy scarlet T-shirt and slim cotton drawstring trews. The freshly laundered uniforms were all kept at the office. She would change there as usual.

Her mind ticked off all the extra equipment they would need for the baby: a neo-natal incubator compatible with the aircraft, pneumatic anti-shock trousers if the mother was haemorrhaging, intravenous fluids and volume expanders.

For once her little car behaved like a dream, as if it knew the importance of the mission. It was barely light in the cool dawn as she slid into the car park reserved for AAMS and raced across to the stores. The door was open and Carson, in an open-necked navy shirt and white trousers, was already checking off what to take. He glanced at her appearance and wet hair.

'Going off on your hols?' he asked.

'I always put my uniform on here, you know that. In case I have to change a tyre.'

'Stay casual for the long flight—you'll be more comfortable. Collect your uniform and help me get this stuff aboard.'

Kirstie did not miss the tightness in his voice or the grim expression. Where had the laid-back, casual attitude gone? Perhaps it was because it was a baby and he did not like children, though Kirstie realised this was an unfair assumption. Carson was universally considerate and caring with all his patients, young and old. She had not noticed a single case where his attention had been less than whole-hearted.

So what was upsetting him about this mission? Suddenly it came to her that he thought they might lose the baby, that the little scrap had a poor chance of surviving the flight. Her heart felt heavy with love and compassion.

She stood still, devouring the strong outline of his shoulders and back. Sometimes she could not take her eyes off him, nor could she stop thinking about him. Heavens, she breathed, her eyes closed, she must be going insane!

Kirstie stowed away the extra equipment and hung up her uniform in the crew locker. She was grateful for being allowed to stay in her own clothes; she was always worried about spilling something on a clean uniform. She checked her face in a small hand mirror. Her eyes were shining, her skin dewy and without make-up, full of mystery and radiance. It was a love-soft face and she was amazed at the change.

Once the jet was through the blanket of clouds and soaring into the clear bright blue hemisphere, she was able to sit down and go through the files. Baby Wallace (m) was two days old; respiratory malfunction.

'The parents are resident in the South of Oman,' said Carson. 'There's a very good three-hundred bed hospital in Salalah, a modern city right on the coast. Although it has excellent paediatric care, it can't deal with every emergency or have the full range of modern equipment. And the temperature at this time of year is killing, high and humid. Mr and Mrs Wallace think the baby has a better chance of survival at Great Ormond Street.'

'Will the hospital accept the baby on our return?'

'Apparently so. They're having one of their rare lulls and have an incubator spare in the neo-natal unit.'

He was so unlike his usual calm self. Kirstie did not know what to make of it. He was drumming his fingers impatiently on the file cover, unable to relax. Even his hair looked as if he had run his fingers through it a dozen times.

Kirstie was out of her depth. His problems were beyond her. She had her own. Kate's wedding loomed close, and, although she had accepted the invitation, she did not yet know if she would have the courage to attend.

She stifled a yawn, hiding the anguish of how little she meant to Carson. 'I think I'll kick off my shoes and catch up on some sleep. It was only five a.m. when you called.'

He darted an odd glance at her, as if she were speaking in a foreign tongue. The cabin tilted round her, not just emotionally but in reality. The plane was making a turn.

'Kirstie, will you let me look at your feet?' he said suddenly.

Kirstie stopped wrestling with the small head pillow

and looked at the melancholy doctor with apprehension and a terrible, aching need. Perhaps she had not heard him properly. 'My feet? Why? Isn't this a little improper?'

'Your feet, my dear. Those two appendages at the end of your legs, that are more often than not shoeless. I've noticed that you take off your shoes at every opportunity.'

His eyes were dangerously impelling. All her barriers began to melt; she was helpless when he showed a personal interest in her.

'Nursing is very tiring, standing on them all day,' she said defensively, her long lashes covering the truth in her eyes. 'I don't mind a purely medical once-over as long as you're not making fun of me. There's nothing wrong with them, no corns, no bunions, nothing ingrowing. I'm not a midnight dancer.'

Carson went down on his haunches, pushing up his sleeves, and took each foot in turn into his hands. She had slender, pretty-shaped feet and he noticed the pearly pink nail varnish on her toenails. Her toes were absurdly sweet; it was all he could do to stop himself from taking the straight little things into his mouth to see if they tasted as sweet.

Kirstie did not know where to look as Carson gently handled her feet, checking the instep, the rotation of ankle, reflexes, alignment of toes. She felt a wild confusion exploding through her body as she sought more of his touch. Small quivers of sensation fluttered in her stomach. She wriggled her toes, mesmerised by the pleasure of his touch, wishing his hands would stroke her legs, caress her ankles, knead the tension from her calves, find other sensitive places to delight.

She was scandalised at the way she was turning to liquid at his touch. It pleasured and embarrassed her at the same time. She knew if they ever lay tangled together, the same response would be a hundredfold and she would allow him bold and possessive liberties. His hand rested intimately on her slender ankle, a thumb stroking down her instep with a delicate but tender touch.

'I think there might p-possibly be something wrong with my neck too,' she joked hopefully. At that moment, the first officer came through from the flight deck and raised his eyebrows at the touching scene.

'What's all this?' he grinned. 'Checking the equipment?'

'Staff clinic,' drawled Carson. 'Any aches and pains dealt with on the spot. No charge for genuine ailments.'

'Have I got a genuine ailment?' Kirstie asked, peering at what seemed to her to be a perfectly ordinary pair of feet.

Carson put them down side by side on the carpeted floor, aligning them exactly, his mind struggling against the alluring honey of her skin, inflamed by the desire sweeping through him. His eyes darkened, hiding their hunger. 'There's nothing wrong with your feet, both rather attractive as feet go, except for one thing.'

Kirstie looked alarmed. Her feet often hurt; it went with the job. She put it down to all the standing.

'They're not both the same size. If you measure them exactly when you get home, you'll find I'm right.'

'But that's nonsense,' said Kirstie. 'Of course they're the same size—I would have noticed.'

'Why should you? Most people only look at one foot at a time when they're putting on a shoe. Then they look at both feet when they're shod. For years you've been squashing one foot into a shoe that's too small and walking tensely to compensate for the discomfort. What size do you take?'

'Five.'

'You probably need a five for the left foot and five-and-a-half for the right.'

'Do you mean I've got to buy two pairs of identical shoes in future, in order to be comfortable?'

'Or find someone with the opposite problem and swop odd shoes,' he grinned. 'You could buy the half size larger and put an inner sole in the left foot. That might work.'

Carson was smiling at her. She had never felt so drawn to the man; it was appalling and awesome. He was irresistible. She longed to push the hair from his forehead, to touch that full, sweet mouth with her finger, to breathe against the silky softness of his strong neck.

'Thank you very much, Doctor, for your advice,' she managed to say. 'Do I throw out my entire collection of shoes?'

'They're your feet,' he said, getting up and dusting off his knees. 'No sense in storing up trouble for the future.'

He rested back in the seat behind Kirstie and closed his eyes to her silvery hair. He wanted no more distraction, and those moments of intimacy had been too disturbing. He had been up half the night, called out by staff at Carey's Yard. An old fellow had fallen on the pavement and broken his hip. He had refused to be taken to hospital until his 'Doc' had seen him.

Carson had gone with him in the ambulance and seen him settled into the novelty of a hospital bed. It was a femur break and would have to be reduced. His hip would be plated and pinned, and there was nothing they could do till the morning.

Carson gave him a pain-killing injection to make sure he got a good night's sleep.

'Blimey, Doc,' said the old man, 'look at these clean sheets! Almost worth breaking my flaming hip. Wotcha say this place was called? The Hilton?'

In minutes Carson was asleep, his long legs stuck out into the aisle. Kirstie fetched a small pillow and eased it under his head. He sighed and shifted to another position. He looked so uncomfortable, but there was nothing she could do. She did not want to wake him and suggest that he slept on the stretcher; it might be a foolhardy reminder of that flight back from Agra.

They came down to refuel in Qurum/Seeb, the airport outside the capital of Muscat, then flew the last lap of the journey to the southern coast and the new city of Salalah. They had flown through a time zone and here the sun was rising on the stony desert, the first rays turning the vastness of greys and browns into shades of ochre and burnt vanilla, before the fullness of the sun painted the whole desert plain an eye-scorching white.

They flew over the escarpment of Jeb Qara, the shelving mountains deeply eroded by wadis and covered in scrub bushes. The narrow coastal strip and fringe of beach ran the length of the plain.

The airport of Saleeb was a short distance from the city. A car was waiting on the tarmac to take them immediately to Quboos Hospital. Already the streets were busy with Arab merchants opening their shuttered shops or setting up stalls in the souk. Strings of camels trod the dust disdainfully, their loads swaying with each step. Veiled women carried produce to the market places on their heads.

Kirstie exclaimed at the unexpected sight of lush

coconut groves and banana plantations; gardens of bougainvillaea and flame trees shaded single-storey villas along the coastal road. They passed the two octagonal gateposts of Al-Hisn palace, the old Sultan's residence on the seashore. Close by was the vegetable souk selling papaw, aubergines, ladies' fingers, water-melon, passion-fruit. The early morning fish souk was a bustle of fishermen emptying their catches of abalone and prawns, large yellow-fin tuna, jackfish, red snap-per, small mountains of silvery sardines.

'It's monsoon country,' said Carson, while pointing out some of the traditional two-storey houses in the narrow side-streets. They were built of limestone with distinctive carved wooden shutters which opened in four sections, designed for the shy womenfolk to peer through. 'The plain of Salalah gets torrential rain and flash floods.'

'Not while we're here, I hope,' said Kirstie.

She noticed the beautifully patterned 'lahaf' head-cloths worn by the women. Some wore a black abbaya over their hair to protect it from the dust which blew constantly. The humidity was already rising oppressively.

The car slowed as they drove past a stunning olive-skinned Omani woman who walked like a Bedouin princess in a tunic of bright silver-braided material over simple black trousers.

'I bet her bride price is high,' said Carson.

'Bride price?' queried Kirstie.

'Brides are expensive. They have to be paid for. The government has been trying to stop it—inflation, you know.'

'Medieval, you know,' said Kirstie.

'It's the custom, but the Omani women have more equality than in many countries. Every profession is open to them. It's equal pay, full legal status, yet great respect is shown to women and, in return, a woman respects her husband. She even asks his permission to go out. She asks out of respect, not out of fear or obedience. You can understand the difference?'

Was he making a pointed reference to her slight difficulty with professional deference? She decided not to commit herself. 'I need to think about it,' she parried.

The humidity hung like a damp net in the air despite the sea breeze. By the time they reached the modern Qaboos Hospital, Kirstie's T-shirt was clinging to her back. Carson's shirt was dark with perspiration and he was only too pleased to meet a tall Omani doctor in the air-conditioned reception area.

'*Ahlan wa sahlan*,' said the doctor in traditional welcome.

'*Ahlan beek*,' Carson replied formally.

'I hope you have had a comfortable journey,' Dr Sayyid's grave smile included Kirstie. 'We're glad to see you. I'll tell you about Baby Wallace as we go to the paediatric intensive care unit.'

'You've a superb hospital,' said Carson, thinking of the basic clinic he had set up at Carey's Yard with such difficulty.

'We're very proud of our facilities,' said Dr Sayyid. 'Perhaps you will have time to look around while you're here. I fear the baby's condition is not stable enough for him to be moved yet.'

It seemed that, like most expatriates, Mrs Wallace had planned to return home to have her baby. But the infant had decided to arrive early, rather too early. He was premature with poorly developed vital centres and respiratory problems. The baby was in an incubator, receiving carefully monitored oxygen, intubated with the endotracheal tube being suctioned. When he was born the amniotic fluid had been clearly stained with meconium and had been successfully aspirated.

'His pulse is feeble,' explained Dr Sayyid. 'He is too delicate to move, but, of course, the parents are anxious to get him away from this terrible heat. His temperature is carefully controlled at all times, but power cuts are always a worry.'

The baby was a tiny, wizened scrap of pink flesh tinged with blue, naked, connected to tubes and drips through his nose and mouth and stick-thin arms. Kirstie's heart kindled with compassion. Babies were so vulnerable, and this little one clung precariously to the thread of life.

Carson examined the baby thoroughly, noted the measures taken, then asked to see Mrs Wallace. She was a woman in her late thirties, tanned with sun-streaked hair, sitting in a cane chair in a loose robe, an unread book on her lap.

'At last—you're here!' she said immediately she saw Carson and Kirstie. 'How soon can we go? This heat is no good for my baby. I want to get to London.'

Carson pulled up another chair and took her hands into his own.

'First we must have a talk, Mrs Wallace,' he said. 'We must do only what is best for your baby. We'll have to monitor his respiratory function constantly. This is done by taking a speck of blood from baby's heel and putting it in a computer. The result tells us the blood gases, and from this we can calculate the amount of oxygen to give him.'

'But you can fly him home,' said Mrs Wallace. 'My baby will be safe with you.'

Kirstie withdrew tactfully. Carson needed to draw on all his tact and charm. Dr Sayyid displayed his own perfect manners by showing her to a staff-room, offering her a cool drink or coffee. It was an airy room with big windows looking out on to well-watered gardens of palms and flowering shrubs, the air-conditioning unit pounding. It was furnished with flower-patterned chairs, low tables with new magazines.

'This is very pleasant and comfortable,' said Kirstie, accepting an iced fruit juice. 'And a fabulous hospital. I'm almost tempted to apply for a job.'

'You would be doing us a favour,' said Dr Sayyid with a swift smile. 'Staffing is a constant problem. I could give you a job tomorrow.'

'I don't understand why. This part of the country is beautiful.'

'Loneliness, homesickness, the heat, everything being strange—it's understandable why people don't stay. Now, if you will excuse me. . .?'

'*Itfaddal*,' said Kirstie, which meant 'please, go ahead', a slang phrase. He looked at her curiously. 'I learned a little Arabic on Mecca flights,' she added with that glorious smile of hers which could melt any grave surgeon's heart. '*Shukran*.'

Dr Sayyid left the staff-room, visibly shaken.

A long time later, Carson reappeared. He flopped into a chair beside Kirstie and she, forgetting all her feminist views, fetched him an iced drink without thinking. He tossed it down with a brief nod of thanks and held the glass out for a refill.

'Mrs Wallace has agreed to wait twenty-four hours,' he told her. 'We couldn't move that baby now—far too risky. I want to see a stabilised heart-rate and respiration. She's very upset, of course.'

'Would you like me to go and see her?'

'Yes, perhaps you'll be able to say something that

I've missed. Then come back here, I want to talk to you.'

Kirstie slipped away, her heart thudding. He wanted to talk to her. What could that mean? Was he going to persuade her to take on head of nursing? She knew Lynda was not making a complete success of the job. Or was he going to ask her to leave? Lynda had been furious after the Austrian mission, accusing Kirstie of usurping her authority and not being one bit grateful for the autographs for her sons.

She found Mrs Wallace weeping into a box of tissues. Kirstie took her along to see her baby in the neo-natal intensive care unit, explaining in detailed but simple terms just why it was too dangerous to move him yet. She was sure that Carson had been through it all already, but coming from another woman it sounded different. Mrs Wallace began to ask questions. She was an intelligent woman and anxious to understand her baby son's problems.

'Could I stay with him a little while?' she asked wistfully. 'Perhaps they'd let me help look after him?'

'I'll ask the sister in charge,' said Kirstie. 'I'm sure it'll be all right. We always used to welcome mothers. Bonding can take place even if you just stroke his skin, or hold his little hand.'

'I'd like to do that,' said Mrs Wallace.

Carson was waiting outside in the cool, airy corridor. He took her arm. 'Sister Duvall, the miracle worker!'

'I'm not coming back with you,' she teased. 'I've fallen in love with this place. I'm going to take any job that's offered to me. Perhaps the Sultan would like a private nurse for the ladies of his harem.'

'Private nursing? Tut, tut, Sister. Against all your high principles, surely?' he said, marching her away.

'What makes you think he wouldn't recruit you for his harem?'

'I'm far too bossy.'

'But Arabs adore fair-haired women.'

'Please stop talking about me as if I'm a commodity!'

He steered her out of the reception area into a waiting car. The dark-skinned driver looked at him expectantly.

'Holiday Inn,' said Carson. '*Min fadlak.*'

'A Holiday Inn?' Kirstie echoed. 'Here?'

'Amazing, isn't it? We've a twenty-four-hour stop-over, so I've booked two rooms. We could both do with a night's sleep.'

'I've only my overnight bag,' she protested.

'That's all you'll need,' he said, putting an end to the conversation.

The Holiday Inn was a newly built hotel seven kilometres outside Salalah. It was designed in brash newness, with many traditional Arab touches, cool archways and intricate filigree work. Kirstie fell on the bed in her air-conditioned room and groaned with relief. She would have a sleep, then a swim from the beach or in the pool. She had been told that the sea swimming could be dangerous at certain times of the year. At least she had her bikini with her and a change of undies.

She slept for an hour and woke fully refreshed. There was a complimentary apricot-coloured towelling bathrobe hanging in the bathroom, so she changed into her bikini, then, modestly covered by the knee-length robe, wandered out to the pool. The midday sun glared down and the pool was deserted. No mad dogs or Englishmen around, she smiled to herself.

She swam a few lengths and then flopped over on to her back, floating lazily, her eyes closed against the dazzling sun. Richmond was a million miles away. She did not care if she ever saw Sean again, she thought with sudden clarity. She had recovered from that insane infatuation. Her pride had been hurt more than her heart. Vanity, thy name is surely woman, she misquoted. She had been hurt because Sean had seen her as nothing more than a little fun at a party, no one special, nothing lasting. It was the fresh-faced, innocent Kate he wanted as a wife. Kirstie's London glamour was worthless to him. And he was so right, thought Kirstie, forgiving him and understanding. Looks and glamour had no value in a true relationship. There was so much more. . .companionship, understanding, laughter, caring. . .

'Feeling better?' asked Carson, splashing alongside her, water streaming from his rugged face, the pirate look returning for an instant.

'It's lovely,' she said, treading water, absurdly happy that he was beside her.

'You've been looking a bit peaky.'

'Overwork, long hours, lack of sleep,' she said flippantly. He was swimming in lazy circles round her and they had the pool to themselves, the aquamarine water sparkling in the sunlight.

'Will you have dinner with me tonight?' asked Carson suddenly.

'Another Carey's Yard?'

'No, not Carey's Yard, I promise. They have an excellent seafood restaurant at the hotel.'

'I've nothing to wear,' Kirstie protested.

'Wear your uniform—there's nothing wrong with it. I'm going back to the hospital this afternoon to keep an eye on that baby, take another blood test. Are you coming with me?'

'Of course. Mrs Wallace is our patient too.' She

climbed out of the pool, water cascading off her slim body, every contour taut and proud and tantalising. She felt his hand clamp round her ankle, pulling her off balance. With a shriek, she fell back into the water, struggling to the surface.

'You didn't ask my permission to leave the pool,' he growled ferociously as he pulled her against him.

'Let me go!' she spluttered. 'This is Arab country—we'll be publicly whipped or something! Cavorting in public isn't allowed. Please, Carson, let me go.'

'Reluctantly,' he said with a sigh. 'Cavorting is delicious, especially with a wet mermaid.'

Kirstie climbed out of the pool, wishing her bikini were not quite so small, but she was soon covered by the robe. Carson followed her, his brief navy shorts clinging to his hips, his muscular legs still brown from walking in India. Her heart turned over every time she saw him.

'Will you come to a wedding with me?' she blurted out, realising straight away that she could have worded it more clearly. He raised his dark eyebrows questioningly.

'My sister's wedding,' she went on quickly. 'It's in July, in Cumbria. The invitation says to bring a friend, and I've no one to take.'

'Poor friendless, overworked nurse,' he teased, then became aware of the pain clouding her hazel eyes. Was this the reason for the reticence, the way Kirstie would suddenly withdraw from the world and surround herself with a prickly, unscalable wall? Sibling jealousy seemed unlikely. Kirstie was a well-balanced person despite this aura of secret hurt.

'I'd be honoured,' he said with old-fashioned courtesy. 'Suit or tails?'

'Just a suit,' said Kirstie, relieved there was to be no

probing. 'I'll give you the details when we get back. We'll drive up. My car, of course.'

'No, my car,' he said firmly. 'I don't fancy a breakdown on a motorway. Perhaps we could call in on my sister, or stay with her overnight. She'd like that.'

'I planned to return the same day,' she told him.

'No again. We'll make it a weekend off.'

'You're so bossy!' Kirstie flung at him.

'I'm so sensible,' he reasoned.

They spent the afternoon with mother and baby. The wee scrap was holding his own; in fact Carson thought there was a slight improvement in the baby's breathing. His colour was better, the bluish tinge less obvious and the computer results showed an improvement.

'What are you going to call him?' asked Kirstie, taking Mrs Wallace along the corridor to visit her baby again.

'Alisdair Cameron,' she said. 'After his grandfather.'

'A grand name for such a mite,' Kirstie laughed. 'But he'll grow into it.'

Helping Mrs Wallace express her milk was a long and tiresome process, but best for the baby. All Kirstie really wanted later was a sandwich and a swim, but Carson had said supper, so she had better be ready. She let herself into her cool room at the Holiday Inn, and was about to collapse on the bed when she saw the parcel. It was wrapped in tissue-thin brown paper and tied with string.

She tore off the paper and folds of silvery blue material fell into her hands. She shook it out and the shimmering gentian-blue silk became a slim caftan with an intricate Arabic pattern on a paler background interwoven with silver thread. The silk was so fine that Kirstie reckoned she could have threaded it through a ring. A second hastily wrapped parcel inside produced a pair of flat, silver-thonged slippers.

She sat on the bed, hugging the gown, happiness flooding through her, saying Carson's name over and over again. How kind, how thoughtful; how simple, how right. The evening ahead was suddenly full of magic and promise. Perhaps he would not ride off with her into the desert, but she hoped he had something equally romantic in mind.

She showered and changed, brushing her hair till it shone in a silver halo. Her skin was faintly tanned and needed little more than eye make-up, but she dabbed expensive perfume all over till she smelt like a harem.

Carson met her in the lounge, still in his white trousers and navy shirt, but somehow, with the magic of the East, they had been laundered and pressed. He'd been swimming and his hair was darkly wet. He rose, his eyes going slowly over her.

'You look beautiful,' he said.

'Thank you,' she smiled. 'And thank you for the caftan. It's perfect. I don't know how you found time——'

'I didn't—Mrs Sayyid went shopping for me. I thought only another woman would know what to buy.'

The pang of disappointment was quickly thrust aside. 'At least you knew my shoe size.'

'Comes in handy,' he said, leading her to the restaurant.

Their sides touched as they strolled into the cool and spacious dining-room. There were flowers everywhere, back-lit glass models and the distant sound of the Arabian Sea. The sun was setting quickly as it did in the Middle East and in minutes the sky would be inky black, dotted with brilliant stars.

'Let's eat,' said Carson, deliberately putting space between them. 'Neither of us had any lunch.'

'Nor breakfast,' Kirstie reminded him.

She barely knew what she ate, but it was a far cry from scrambled eggs—a cold soup, local lobster with salad, exotic fruits with cream from the Royal farm at Arzat. They did not touch alcohol, which was available in the hotel, because they were both technically on duty and the eight-hour ban before flying stood. But the iced fruit juice was delicious and they took their coffee out on to the terrace, sitting on cane chairs in the sultry evening warmth.

'It's like velvet,' said Kirstie, gazing up at the glowing night sky. 'And the stars are like diamonds.'

'No pollution,' said Carson, unable to take his eyes off her vibrant face. 'We've got layers of ozone rubbish between us and our night sky. It's like looking through mud. Would you like a last walk along the beach before I go back to the hospital to check on Baby Wallace? I want to see if his improvement is holding up. If so, I'd like to leave very early in the cool of the morning.'

He took her hand and led her through the flowering gardens, taking the path to the beach. The scent of bougainvillaea was almost overpowering, petals brushing against her skin. The silvery arc of sand stretched unbroken into the distance, unspoilt and empty.

'Mind the crabs,' said Carson.

'What?' Kirstie jumped back.

'The sand is swarming with crabs. . .' he chuckled '. . .at dawn.'

She knew he was going to kiss her. She would not stop him. She could not. She loved him, and her body longed for the strong feel of his arms. His kiss was only a breath away and time stood still.

# CHAPTER EIGHT

CARSON'S arms tightened round Kirstie, hands moving down to the small of her back, tracing her spine through the thin silk, coming to rest on her small, tight buttocks. She gasped at the intimacy of the touch and as his mouth found her lips, fiercely and more demanding than ever before, arousing her mouth to open to his tongue.

She could feel her breasts swelling with desire as she pressed herself against him, fingers deep in his hair, hips hard against his thighs.

You're giving yourself away, a small voice warned, but Kirstie did not care. She was beyond caring. This moment, here and now, was all that mattered—this marvellously beautiful man, this loving, this experience, this tumultuous feeling sweeping through her.

A long sigh left her as he began to mouth her neck with small, delicate butterfly kisses, as exquisitely gentle as anything she had ever felt before. She arched her neck so that he could find his way to every sensitive spot.

'Kirstie, you're so lovely. I can't stop kissing you. I want to kiss every inch of your lovely body,' he said huskily.

Kirstie clung to him, feeling quite faint at the thought of such bliss. How was she ever going to come to her senses in this haze of passion? She put her hands on the hard curve of his hips, pulling him against her until there was nowhere else to go. She was being scandalously wanton and she did not care.

Carson tilted her chin upwards, his face darkly etched in the moonlight, his eyes glowing with a primitive intensity. He could endure no more of the tantalising delay. It was against sense, against reason to deny the pulsating longing that they felt for each other.

Kirstie was conscious of a sudden, alien tug at the roots of her hair. 'Ouch!' she shuddered.

'Sorry, darling,' he murmured. 'Your hair's caught in my ring.' She stood still, trembling while he tried to disentangle it. 'This damned ring—the claws are so sharp. I stopped wearing it for years because it kept catching on things. Then for some reason I put it on again this morning. . . There, it's free. Sorry.' He pretended to examine her head. 'No damage, no bald patches. You can't sue me.'

Kirstie was staring at his ring, a gold signet ring, a dark gemstone held in an intricate setting. 'It's still loose on your finger,' she said numbly.

'I ought to get it fixed. It was my grandfather's. . .still loose? What do you mean?'

'I'm only saying that you ought to have a licence for that ring.' Her voice rose in agitation. 'It's a dangerous weapon. One day you could hurt somebody.'

She knew him now. The clouds parted and she saw him as clearly as she had momentarily all those years ago. Different, younger, smooth-faced, only his bed-side manner a little rough at the edges.

She started to walk rapidly back to the hotel, tripping as she hurried, bunching the long caftan in her hands, fighting against the tears.

'Hold on there, Kirstie! I only caught my ring in your hair. Heavens, you lost six hairs at the most! Is that a disaster?'

'Meeting you again is the disaster,' she said stonily.

'I thought I knew you, but you'd changed and it was a long time ago. Goodnight, Dr Black. Thank you for the nice supper,' she added like a polite child.

'What do you mean, goodnight, Dr Black?' Carson pulled her back angrily. 'What on earth are you talking about? When did we meet? You can't just leave like that!'

'Yes, I can. Just watch me. I'm going.'

'Dammit, woman, you're the most infuriating creature I've ever come across!' He swore again and turned sharply on his heels, both hands rising in a supplication to Allah for patience. She heard his footsteps going in the direction of the beach.

'Mind the crabs!' she shouted to the darkness, catching the sob in her voice.

She slept restlessly. At this rate she would end up being a patient, not the nurse. She would put heat exhaustion on the form. She could hardly put 'post-trauma from bad experience Mid-Atlantic plus broken heart'. Lynda Marshall would be down on her, wielding her blackest Biro.

The five a.m. call came on her room phone and Kirstie went into top gear. By six a.m. they were airborne, Baby Wallace safely in his incubator, still wired up to everything in sight. But he was a pinker colour and almost ready to breathe on his own. Mrs Wallace wept tears of relief as the plane soared into the sky, but also tears of sadness for leaving her husband behind in Salalah.

Carson was cool towards Kirstie, reserving his warmth and kindness for dealing with the mother and baby. His comments to her were purely professional.

'Please monitor the oxygen carefully,' he said quite

unnecessarily. 'Too much can be as harmful as too little.'

'Yes, Doctor,' she said, knowing perfectly well that too much oxygen could blind a premature baby.

'Check the tube for blockages. We may have to give him some epinephrine in solution. You could prepare a dose in case: 0.1 ml per kilogram of birth weight.'

'Yes, Doctor.'

She moved like an automaton. She had behaved stupidly, but realising who he was at last had come as a nasty shock, just when she was feeling vulnerable and awash with love. Seeing the ring again had shattered her composure. All she could think of was the humiliating scene on the Boeing 747 and the heavy signet ring striking her across the face. She touched the scar under her hair. Carson's mark. He had marked her for sure, and not just on her face.

'Sister! Are you with us? I've had to speak to you twice. Would you help Mrs Wallace? She's somewhat distressed.'

Mrs Wallace had a very normal reluctance to use the plane's tiny toilet facility while in the air. It was claustrophobic. She was also feeling slightly airsick. Kirstie took her along to the toilet, waiting outside while Mrs Wallace coped in the confined space, refusing to close the door. The new mother was perspiring and yawning when she emerged, taking little interest in anything.

Kirstie made her comfortable in a semi-recumbent position, directing a ventilator jet on to Mrs Wallace's pale face. She kept up a steady conversation of trivialities to distract the woman while she took her blood pressure and pulse. Then Kirstie made a sweet drink for her to sip and gave her a tablet of quick-acting meclozine to chew.

'Why not close your eyes?' said Kirstie. 'The tablet will probably make you feel sleepy.'

Such was the power of suggestion that Mrs Wallace was soon dozing lightly. As soon as she awoke there would be milk to draw off to give the baby. When they came down to refuel, Mrs Wallace took advantage of the break to stretch her legs and appreciate a cooler climate.

'What an interesting job you have,' she said to Kirstie. 'You get to all these exciting places.'

'But I don't get to see much of these exciting places unless there's a stop-over. I've had enough airports to last a lifetime. I'm thinking of returning to hospital work. I've already been offered a job that would be a change.'

'Don't do anything hasty,' said Mrs Wallace. 'You might end up in Salalah as I did!'

Kirstie laughed. She had been thinking of Dr Sayyid's offer if working with Carson became impossible. 'That would be a surprise.'

'What would be a surprise, Sister?' asked Carson, his face grim in the sunlight, eyes glinting dangerously blue. 'I know you're full of surprises.'

Kirstie flushed, annoyed that he should try and embarrass her in front of their patient. It was not fair or ethical. She gave him a carefully controlled glare.

'Mrs Wallace would like some privacy on the plane,' she said, the sweetness of her tone belying the stoniness in her eyes. 'I'll fix up a screen. Her milk production is heading for overtime, a somewhat painful condition.'

'I'm such a nuisance,' sighed Mrs Wallace.

'Perfectly natural,' said Carson, aware that Kirstie had ignored his question. 'Allow me to assist with the screen.'

He helped her with icy politeness, the atmosphere horribly strained. But Kirstie knew, for her patient's sake, she must not allow any inkling to reach Mrs Wallace or destroy her confidence in them as a team.

'Thank you, Doctor,' she said, as normally as possible.

It was the smallest passenger on board who took the situation into his own tiny hands. He must have sensed he was on his way home or perhaps it was the result of the hours of gentle mother-stroking, but he began to improve dramatically. The worry visibly lifted from Carson's face. Mrs Wallace wept again. Even the flight crew came out to visit the baby sleeping in his incubator, his breath like sweet flowers.

'We could almost have him breathing on his own,' said Carson jubilantly. 'But I shan't risk it. I'm sure he could do it, but I'll let Great Ormond Street decide.'

The pilot made a smooth landing at Heathrow. There was not only an ambulance waiting but two joyous grandparents. Mrs Wallace burst into more tears.

A wheelchair was waiting for Mrs Wallace at the hospital. She pulled a face as Kirstie tucked another blanket round her. 'I'd forgotten about the awful English weather,' she said. 'How can I ever thank you, Sister Duvall? You've been like a real sister to me. I hope we meet again.'

'I'm sure we shall,' said Kirstie, giving her hand a squeeze. 'I shall want to know how Alisdair Cameron is getting on.'

'And best of luck with that new job,' Mrs Wallace waved as she was wheeled into the hospital.

'What new job?' asked Carson brusquely. 'You haven't mentioned it to me. If you're thinking of leaving us, I trust you'll give the required four weeks' notice.'

It was as if he had never known her, never held her in his arms. He was a cold, impersonal stranger.

'I never said——' Kirstie began. 'You're jumping to conclusions.'

'I should also like to be told your reasons for leaving. It can't be for extra money, knowing your well-voiced disapproval of financial gain.'

'You simply overheard a joke,' said Kirstie, determined to get a word in.

'To lose my best nurse would be no joke,' he said tersely, hailing a taxi. 'I hope you know what you're doing.'

'I'm not doing anything, Dr Black. If you'll give me a chance, I'll explain to you.'

But the taxi had drawn up to the kerb. He did not offer to share it with her. He got in, face set with disapproval. Kirstie did not enlighten him further. He had been eavesdropping and it was his own fault if he had jumped to the wrong conclusion.

She watched the taxi drive away, joining the stream of traffic, a glitter of tired tears in her eyes. The distance between them became an impossible void.

Perhaps he was going to Carey's Yard or Thornhill, Kirstie thought miserably as she joined the crowds surging into the underground station. She took the Richmond line in a daze, hoping to be home before it rained again, but when she came out at the station it was pouring. She turned up the collar of her anorak and set out to cover the ten-minute walk as quickly as possible. Soon her hair was plastered to her head, bare hands blue with cold, fingers stiffly clutching her overnight bag.

The flat was welcoming, but she felt as if she had

been away years. She removed the dead flowers and tipped away the stale water. She needed to get her feet firmly back on the ground—all these exotic beaches and international hotels threw a girl off axis. She prescribed a dose of housework to bring herself to her senses. The hum of the vacuum cleaner was like a drug as she polished and cleaned. When everywhere was sparkling and shining to her satisfaction, she made a coffee and a cheese sandwich. Her body clock was completely haywire; she did not know whether she was supposed to be sleeping or eating.

In moments she was asleep in an armchair, exhausted by her exertions, the trauma of the flight and the misery building up in her heart. This was a hundred times worse than the hurt she had suffered through Sean's rejection. She could see now how shallow that had been, how childish her reaction and feelings. This was a devastating gut pain; she felt as if part of her were dying. She had lost the last of her illusions. She wasn't safe to be let out alone.

It took a while for the telephone's ringing to penetrate her thick blanket of sleep. Daylight had almost faded and the sloping ceilings cast unfamiliar shadows across the walls.

'Hello?' she said sleepily.

'Sister Duvall? So you're at home. I thought so.' It was Lynda Marshall. 'I have just been informed of thousands of pounds' worth of expensive aerial incubators and equipment being abandoned in our office with no one to check it or return it to the stores. You apparently decided your duties ended with delivering Mrs Wallace and baby to the hospital. You know perfectly well that the equipment in the plane has to be dismantled before the plane can return to base.'

Kirstie groaned. 'I'm terribly sorry—I quite forgot. I'll come over right away.'

'Don't bother,' Lynda snapped. 'Millie has done it.'

'That's kind of her. Thank you. . .'

The coffee was cold and the sandwich dried out. Kirstie reheated the coffee and toasted the sandwich. She knew she must snap out of this mood before it overwhelmed her. Soon she should shop for a wedding present and a wedding outfit. . .something in unrelieved khaki might be appropriate so she could merge into the background.

She bought the first outfit that fitted. It was all wrong, but Kirstie had no resistance to the assistant who kept saying how wonderful it looked with her hair and hazel eyes. It was a matronly two-piece in olive-green, a colour guaranteed to dim any sparkle she might manage to feel on the day.

She recovered her energy and spirits over the next couple of days, but her thoughts were always with Carson, imagining him at Carey's Yard or immersed in his research at Thornhill Drugs. She wondered who looked after his house at Strand-on-the-Green. Did he have a housekeeper? Suddenly she realised she knew nothing about his private life. There might even be a live-in girlfriend.

Hurriedly she changed into a plain black tracksuit and trainers before the madness could leave her mind. It was a long walk through the Old Deer Park, past Kew Observatory and the pagoda, along the river path to Kew Bridge. She set out at a brisk pace, kidding herself she was getting some much-needed exercise.

The river was busy with pleasure boats steaming up and down, small brown ducks scrabbling at the water's edge, deer grazing beneath the dappled trees. It was so English and so peaceful. Why couldn't she just enjoy it?

She stood outside the row of unspoiled restored houses at Strand-on-the-Green, feeling like an intruder, willowy trees brushing the towpath. Fishermen's cottages was a misnomer. Some were three-storeyed, tastefully renovated, preserved with care. Each had an individuality, emphasised with subtle touches, worn steps, bay windows, balconies. Kirstie wondered which was Carson's house and what on earth she was doing there, hovering like some lovesick teenager for a glimpse of her beloved.

'Coming in for a drink?' called Carson, leaning over from a first-floor balcony, dishevelled and wearing a dark blue bathrobe.

His house was white-fronted, two tall sash windows leading on to the balcony where he stood, another floor above under a black-edged gable.

'Some cottage,' she remarked.

'You know how some estate agents exaggerate,' he grinned. 'Are you coming in? I make a knock-out fruit punch.'

'I thought we weren't speaking,' said Kirstie. 'The last time we met, we certainly weren't speaking.'

'There, and I thought you'd come by to make amends.'

'I certainly have not,' said Kirstie with spirit.

'You're very certain about everything this morning. I like that. Don't move an inch. I'm coming down to let you in. I can't stay mad at you for long, young woman.'

It would have been foolish to try and run away. Kirstie found herself being ushered up a flight of steps, into a cool white-tiled hallway. Carson's hand propelled her firmly.

'We get flooded if there's a surging spring tide,' he said. 'Most of the houses are raised.'

He steered her through a passage from which she glimpsed a modern pine-fitted kitchen, out into a minuscule patio garden. There was just room for a table and two cane chairs fitted with floral cushions. A trellis of roses covered one wall, its fragrance sweet and heady.

Kirstie touched a pale peach petal. 'A Carey's Yard rose?' she asked, remembering the rose on their supper table.

Carson nodded. 'Home-grown.'

'You never cease to surprise me.' She was trying not to look at his bare legs, the dark hair dusting his tanned skin.

'Good. I should hate to be thought boring.'

He went back into the kitchen and she could hear the rattle of ice and the clink of glasses. She lay back in a chair, enjoying the oasis of peace, watching a ladybird stumble across the white table on unsteady legs. Carson seemed to have a knack of creating places in which to refresh himself, first the rooftop and now his own backyard.

A rose had fallen on to the ground. Kirstie scooped the fragile petals into her hand and buried her nose in their fragrance. If only she could store these memories for the lonely times!

Carson returned with two tall glasses filled with a pinky orange drink, topped with sliced strawberries.

'What, no umbrellas?' laughed Kirstie.

'The barman is clean out of umbrellas.' He had changed into jeans and a washed-out shirt, sleeves rolled up to the elbow. He wore his affluence so naturally, it was nothing to do with clothes.

Kirstie took a long drink. It was pleasantly dry.

'Orange juice,' she said on reflection. 'Martini .
Gin? Vodka?'

'What a sophisticated palate!'

'Am I right?'

'I'm not going to tell you. Anyway, I make it differently every time.'

Kirstie smiled, glad she was off duty. She could feel the alcohol trickling into her veins, spreading its warmth insidiously along her limbs. She rested back on the cushion and half closed her eyes, still seeing Carson's dark head through her lashes. He was sprawled in the opposite chair, looking absurdly relaxed and casual. Was this the ogre who could be so infuriating at times?

She knew she ought to go while she could still walk, but everything about the tiny rose-filled garden was lulling her into utter contentment. Surely she was allowed some happiness, enjoying Carson's company in an uncomplicated way.

'Who does all this?' She indicated the flowers.

'I do, when there's the time. I'm a midnight gardener. I come out here when I'm late back from work. It's very therapeutic. The neighbours think I'm crazy.'

'I've got a window-box.'

'We all have to begin small.' He pulled his chair closer, effectively cutting off her escape route through the house. He refilled her glass from a jug. 'Don't look so alarmed, Kirstie. I'm not trying to get you tight, but I do want to talk to you. We must get things straightened out. Ninety per cent of the time we work well together as a team. I value your skills highly, yet you seem to go out of your way to cross swords with me. I can't understand it.'

Kirstie stared down into the pink depths of the drink, at a loss for a reply. How could she tell him that she was blindly in love with him, spellbound and helpless, fighting the feelings with every ounce of her strength?

'I can understand your disapproval of my financial involvement with AAMS, and with Thornhill Drugs. It makes no difference to my ability as a doctor. There's more to medicine than the hard slog of a GP or hospital registrar. Or perhaps that's what you would rather see me doing?'

'No,' said Kirstie in a small voice.

'Then for goodness' sake, woman, tell me what else it is that I'm doing wrong? Is it because I've kissed you? God knows, Kirstie, I can't help it. You're so kissable, so lovely. . .yet so remote. I can't keep my hands off you. If you find it offensive, then I'll try harder to keep a distance.'

'No, it's not that.' Kirstie's voice was so low, he had to lean forward to catch what she was saying. He was torn between impatience at her attitude and a yearning for her to understand his point of view.

'What is it, then? We always seem to be getting on so well, then suddenly I put my big feet in it and you're off, nose in the air, voice coated in icicles, freezing me out.'

'Do I do that?' she asked, stricken. Carson leaned forward, took away the glass, enclosing her hands in a warm grasp.

'Remember Salalah? We were having a perfect evening together, but the moment I began to kiss you everything was shot to pieces. I just don't understand it.'

Carson's face was so forlorn and dismayed, dark eyebrows drawn together, that Kirstie knew she was going to have to tell him. She looked back at him, hazel eyes pleading for understanding and tolerance.

'Orange juice,' she said on reflection. 'Martini Rosso. Gin? Vodka?'

'What a sophisticated palate!'

'Am I right?'

'I'm not going to tell you. Anyway, I make it differently every time.'

Kirstie smiled, glad she was off duty. She could feel the alcohol trickling into her veins, spreading its warmth insidiously along her limbs. She rested back on the cushion and half closed her eyes, still seeing Carson's dark head through her lashes. He was sprawled in the opposite chair, looking absurdly relaxed and casual. Was this the ogre who could be so infuriating at times?

She knew she ought to go while she could still walk, but everything about the tiny rose-filled garden was lulling her into utter contentment. Surely she was allowed some happiness, enjoying Carson's company in an uncomplicated way.

'Who does all this?' She indicated the flowers.

'I do, when there's the time. I'm a midnight gardener. I come out here when I'm late back from work. It's very therapeutic. The neighbours think I'm crazy.'

'I've got a window-box.'

'We all have to begin small.' He pulled his chair closer, effectively cutting off her escape route through the house. He refilled her glass from a jug. 'Don't look so alarmed, Kirstie. I'm not trying to get you tight, but I do want to talk to you. We must get things straightened out. Ninety per cent of the time we work well together as a team. I value your skills highly, yet you seem to go out of your way to cross swords with me. I can't understand it.'

Kirstie stared down into the pink depths of the drink, at a loss for a reply. How could she tell him that she was blindly in love with him, spellbound and helpless, fighting the feelings with every ounce of her strength?

'I can understand your disapproval of my financial involvement with AAMS, and with Thornhill Drugs. It makes no difference to my ability as a doctor. There's more to medicine than the hard slog of a GP or hospital registrar. Or perhaps that's what you would rather see me doing?'

'No,' said Kirstie in a small voice.

'Then for goodness' sake, woman, tell me what else it is that I'm doing wrong? Is it because I've kissed you? God knows, Kirstie, I can't help it. You're so kissable, so lovely. . .yet so remote. I can't keep my hands off you. If you find it offensive, then I'll try harder to keep a distance.'

'No, it's not that.' Kirstie's voice was so low, he had to lean forward to catch what she was saying. He was torn between impatience at her attitude and a yearning for her to understand his point of view.

'What is it, then? We always seem to be getting on so well, then suddenly I put my big feet in it and you're off, nose in the air, voice coated in icicles, freezing me out.'

'Do I do that?' she asked, stricken. Carson leaned forward, took away the glass, enclosing her hands in a warm grasp.

'Remember Salalah? We were having a perfect evening together, but the moment I began to kiss you everything was shot to pieces. I just don't understand it.'

Carson's face was so forlorn and dismayed, dark eyebrows drawn together, that Kirstie knew she was going to have to tell him. She looked back at him, hazel eyes pleading for understanding and tolerance.

'I should have told you this weeks ago,' she began, 'but I was afraid of the consequences. It isn't going to be easy and I don't know where to begin. It was your ring. Seeing it again brought it all back to me.'

With one swift movement, he lifted her out of the chair and on to his lap. He settled her against his chest with a big sigh.

'At last, the truth! Tell me like a story, Kirstie, as if it happened to someone else.'

They were nearing the end of the long haul flight from New York to Heathrow with over three hundred passengers on a Boeing 747, most of them trying to sleep in awkward positions, the cabin lights dimmed to blue. Kirstie was slumped on a crew seat, a beaker of coffee growing cold in her hand. It had been a busy flight with fractious children and demanding mothers. She had been rushed off her feet with extra duties, as well as all the routine meals, drinks and duty-free rounds.

She was not feeling well. Apart from it being the wrong time of the month, she was definitely incubating something. She had hardly slept in New York, alternately tossing hot and shivering cold. If she was going to be ill, she wanted to get home. She could not afford to be sick in New York. Besides, air stewardesses were supposed to be a perpetual picture of glamour and health, never a blemish or sniffy nose. Woe betide any spot that dared to appear!

Kirstie stretched out her legs and closed her eyes, hoping she wouldn't get any more calls before they served breakfast. If she could doze for a few minutes, she might feel better.

Suddenly she jerked upwards. Shouts and screams were coming from the rear passenger section. She tossed her coffee into the sink and ran out, heart sinking.

A man was staggering up the aisle, lurching from side to side, grabbing at people, his face distorted in the half light.

This was all she needed, Kirstie thought, a paralytic drunk in mid-air. Where were the stewards? The man must have been drinking from a hip flask or broken into his duty-free.

She caught his arm politely. 'I think you'd better return to your seat, sir.'

He was a youngish man, shirt-sleeved, tie loosened, brown hair flopping over his forehead. He stared at her, uncomprehending. His arm flew up, catching her a sharp blow on the shoulder. He was shaking violently and twitching, arms flailing. Kirstie thought he was going to attack her and cried out in alarm.

The next moments were total confusion. Several passengers grabbed the man. He was making a terrible noise, clenching his teeth, foam flecking his mouth.

He's gone mad, thought Kirstie, trying to remember her first-aid training. Restrain the passenger, sit on him, protect the other passengers.

He was hitting out in all directions. Children woke up and started to cry, adding to the din. There was pandemonium. A woman nearby was screaming, and Kirstie turned to quieten her.

A man hurried through from the first-class section. In the dim light, Kirstie was only aware of a tall figure with dark, saturnine features. He caught her a sharp blow across the face which knocked all the breath out of her.

'Stop screaming, woman, and do as I say! Get all these people back to their seats. Make room for the man to fall without hurting himself.'

'It wasn't me screaming,' said Kirstie, shocked, but the tall man was not listening. His attention was elsewhere.

The man supported the frenzied passenger as he fell to the floor. He grabbed airline blankets and draped them over any nearby metal or protruding chair supports. Swiftly he moved bags and hand luggage out of the way. The other passengers quietened down, relieved that someone was in control of the situation and knew what he was doing.

Kirstie tried to put a pillow under the young man's head, but the interfering passenger from First Class snatched it away.

'Keep the airway free,' he snapped. 'Didn't they teach you anything?'

When the jerking and twitching stopped, the stranger rolled the now unconscious man over on to his side, checking that his airway was not constricted. He was breathing noisily but without difficulty.

Kirstie, still shocked and upset by the slap, stumbled about her duties like an automaton. Her long silvery hair was falling free from its severe topknot, untidy strands on her shoulders, her make-up smudged with tears.

'Don't you know an epileptic fit when you see one?' the stranger barked at her. He was still kneeling by the man, not doing anything, waiting for the muscles to relax.

'I thought he was drunk or mad,' she faltered. 'But I realise now——'

'The last thing you should do is to restrain an epileptic. They're not dangerous, only to themselves. Just move or cover anything on which they might get hurt.'

'I should have known. . .' She was feeling desperately sick. She had to get away.

'He's coming round. We'll leave him where he is for a few minutes, then perhaps one of the stewards will help me carry him into First Class. He ought to rest quietly for at least an hour. He won't remember anything. He'll probably sleep.'

Kirstie nodded, unable to speak, hardly able to stand straight. She turned away miserably.

'I'm sorry I had to hit you,' he went on, rising, 'but a hysterical woman is no help to anyone, and I needed your help.'

'It wasn't me,' said Kirstie again.

It was only afterwards that she discovered the inch-long cut on her cheekbone. The trickle of blood had dried on her skin like a streak of war-paint.

There was almost complete silence when Kirstie finished her story. A plane droned overhead, an insect buzzed, rose leaves rustled like sad music.

Carson pushed aside her hair and looked at the fine white scar. 'So I did this,' he said. 'Carson's mark.'

'You didn't mean to cut me.'

'This damned ring! I'll never wear it again.'

'You were only trying to control a hysterical woman. It was necessary. I would do the same myself if I had to. Only, in the half-light, you hit the wrong woman.'

Carson was hardly listening. He was tracing the scar with the tip of his finger. 'God, how barbaric! I'll never forgive myself. Kirstie, what can I say? How can I make amends? I did this to you,' he was saying, his voice despairing. 'No wonder you've never trusted me! What can I do?'

'Just try to understand how I felt in Salalah, realising

it was you, knowing that I was only so high in your esteem.'

'But it was years ago, and I didn't recognise you.'

'Not surprising. I had long hair then, all piled up, lashings of make-up, smart uniform. . . Besides, the light was dim and you hardly looked at me.'

'I've a lot of apologising to do,' he said, turning her face towards him, this new closeness so strange and sweet and disturbing. Kirstie did not protest.

'It's all over. Let's forget it,' she tried to say. 'Anyway, I should be grateful. It was because of that incident that I became a nurse, and I've never regretted it.'

He kissed the scar gently and Kirstie wondered how she had lived so long without this man. But common sense told her that any involvement with Carson was dangerous; he would break her heart. He could crush her spirit, reduce her to nothing again. She could not risk being a hostage to love.

Kirstie knew there was only one course left open to her. She had to be free of Carson's powerful hold over her body and her senses. She had to be free of him and allowed to live a life uncomplicated by relationships. It was the only way not to get hurt. She wanted to be heart-free, independent, a woman in her own right.

'Now you know the story, I'm sure you'll understand. I'm sorry, Carson, but I don't think I can work with AAMS any longer. It would be better if I left. I've been offered a job abroad and I may take it.'

Carson's face was only inches away. She saw his eyes darken, the compassion disappear. 'Why? I don't want you to go. Heavens, Kirstie, what's the problem now?'

'I feel it would be better all round. I'm a thorn in Lynda Marshall's side. She'd be pleased to see me go.'

'It doesn't matter what Lynda thinks,' said Carson angrily. 'She doesn't run AAMS. I do, and I want you to stay.'

'No, my mind is made up, Carson. I need a fresh start, breathing space, a new horizon.'

'Nonsense,' he snapped. 'You need me. You need someone like me to love you, make you feel a real woman. That's what you want. Why don't you admit it?'

'Oh my, what an ego! Is there no limit? I need you like I need a sore head, brother.' Despair crept into Kirstie's bones as she heard herself saying exactly the opposite to what she felt about Carson. 'You can have my four weeks' notice right now.'

'If you're quite determined, then I can't stop you, but you're making a mistake. A very stupid mistake,' he said coldly. 'Have you finished your drink? I'll drive you home.' He stood up, practically tipping her off his lap.

'No, thank you,' she said, steadying herself against the table. 'I can walk.'

'Please yourself. I'm due at Carey's Yard in ten minutes.'

'You'd better go, then. I'll let myself out.'

She walked past him, head held high, mouth dry, knowing that everything had gone. She had blown it. As she walked along the cool passage, she noticed for the first time a framed photograph on the antique hall table. It was a photograph of a much younger Carson Black and by his side was a young woman, dark-haired and smiling up at him. But Kirstie's glance was drawn to the child in Carson's arms. A year-old boy with the same electric blue eyes and firm chin.

Kirstie felt a stab of hunger for both father and son, for there could be no doubt. This was Carson's son. Ragged grief surged through her, hurrying her footsteps.

It was not till she was outside that she realised she still held a handful of crushed rose petals. She let them fall into the swirling river, letting the racing water carry them to the sea.

# CHAPTER NINE

THE Lotus was the ideal car for motorway driving, cruising in the fast lane at a steady seventy with Carson pulling over into the centre lane every time he saw a maniac in his rear-view mirror approaching at ninety.

'Madness!' he muttered.

Madness, echoed Kirstie. The last three weeks had been a kind of madness, and it was madness now to be driving to Cumbria with Carson to Kate's wedding. After giving her notice, she had thought the arrangement would be off, but some days later he had approached her in the cool and detached manner he now used for any dealings.

'I've spoken to my sister. She's looking forward to our visit.'

'There's no need——' Kirstie began.

'I see her so rarely. It's an excellent opportunity.'

Kirstie racked her brains to think how she could get out of the commitment. A whole day in Carson's company would be more than she could bear, a punishment for her wanton behaviour. She was being unnecessarily hard on herself, but the less time they were together, the better. Responding to Carson's caresses had been the natural reaction of a woman falling in love.

His attitude had changed. There was no more teasing, no more unexpected gentleness, none of the friendly moments which had become so precious. Every cold remark, every offhand comment, hurt her desperately.

'It's very kind of you to still take me,' she said stiffly.

'I said I would, didn't I? Besides, your car is a motorway hazard; you'd be surrounded by flashing lights and AA vans in no time at all.'

Kirstie did not have the energy to argue with him. She wrapped space around her and departed for the day's mission. It was a messy road accident on the island of Kos and a whole family of four were involved. One of the locum doctors was going with her. Greek traffic accidents were notorious and speed was essential in getting the family home for the right medical treatment.

It was a traumatic mission. All four members of the family had been injured in a horrific road accident. Fortunately the two children, having been in the back of the hired car, had got away with cuts and bruises. But their parents were badly injured. Kirstie tended them on the flight back, wishing she could undo all the wrongs in the world. These young parents would never be the same. It would be months, years even, before they would be able to live a normal life again.

No, never, thought Kirstie, trying to keep the fretful children quiet. Never for her the pain of a family. She looked at the young mother's waxen, shocked face and wondered how she would survive.

Lynda Marshall had mellowed since learning of Kirstie's departure, no longer seeing her as a threat or competition.

'You could have the weekend off for your sister's wedding,' said Lynda. 'I dare say you could do with a break.'

'Thank you,' said Kirstie, subdued. 'If you're sure you can manage.'

'We've a couple of new freelance nurses on the list now. Both very reliable and efficient.'

Kirstie accepted Lynda's hint that she was not going to be missed. A lot of Kirstie's natural spirit had been knocked out of her, despite all her resolutions to be strong. The knowledge that Carson had a wife and child somewhere had been a final blow. They might be separated or divorced, nevertheless they existed and still had a place in his life. Why had he never mentioned them? But why should he? There had never been one word of love pass between them. Kirstie had never been anything more than an attractive member of staff, available and apparently willing to indulge in the odd romantic interlude to enliven a stop-over.

Carson slotted in a cassette of classical guitar music, and the plaintive notes that filled the speeding car matched Kirstie's aching heart.

'Coffee,' he said, breaking an hour-long silence. He slowed down and turned into a service station car park. He shouldered his way through the milling throng and went to an island counter serving drinks. He returned with a tray of coffee and biscuits. Kirstie had meanwhile cleared a table of debris.

'I'm sorry this is so uncivilised, but I need a rest from driving,' Carson apologised.

'Very sensible,' said Kirstie.

They sat in more polite silence. Carson looked darkly handsome in a well-tailored grey suit, pale shirt and grey silk tie. Kirstie yearned for things to be different. If only she had been taking Carson to the wedding as a real friend. . . Instead they were travelling like strangers.

'This is crazy!' he suddenly exploded. 'I can't begin to understand why you're leaving us. What is it about this new job that's so special? What is it? You haven't said a word.'

Kirstie stirred her coffee uneasily. The offer of a job from Dr Sayyid had only been in passing. She had not followed it up. She did not know what she was going to do.

'My reasons are very personal. I can't tell you.'

'I know that Lynda's difficult to get along with. She was trained in the days of scrubbing floors.'

'It's not Lynda,' she told him.

'It must be me, then,' he said curtly, with a sharp intake of breath. 'I suppose you can't stand the sight of me. That does wonders for my confidence! I know I was arrogant and rude on that flight from Agra, but the circumstances were difficult.'

'I shouldn't have thought it mattered in the slightest what I feel about you,' said Kirstie, staring at a group of youngsters larking about in the car park. 'We have nothing in common beyond our work. I can assure you that your attitude to me has in no way influenced my decision to leave.'

'You're lying,' he said, not looking at her. 'Let's get today over, then we needn't see each other again. I'm flying to Paris on Monday to the Pasteur Institute and shall be away several days.'

There was a sudden scuffle by her side, and a youth fell heavily against her shoulder. The coffee cascaded down the front of her dress, the hot liquid stinging her skin.

Carson shot to his feet and grabbed the boy. 'You clumsy idiot! Look what you've done.'

'Sorry, mate,' said the youth, raising his hands in apology. Carson was too big and powerfully built to hassle with. 'Sorry, lady.' He sidled away quickly.

Carson turned to Kirstie. A dark stain was spreading down the front of her dress and over her lap.

'I didn't want to go to the wedding anyway,' said Kirstie. 'We can call it off now. I'll phone.'

'Cold water. Your skin may be burnt.'

'I know,' said Kirstie, heading for the cloakroom. She slipped out of the top of her dress and doused her breasts with splashes of cold water. The material had protected her skin. It was not burnt, only red. She tried to rinse the coffee out of the dress, but that only seemed to make matters worse, and the ugly brown stain spread in all directions.

She stared at herself in the mirror. She had never looked so awful. Her face was strained with tension. Her make-up had disappeared. There was no way she was going to let her family see her looking like this.

She marched out of the cloakroom, head high. Carson was leaning against his car.

'I look like a stagnant pond,' she said. 'We can't go. It's all off.'

'I thought Sister Duvall could cope with anything. Get in,' he said, opening the door.

'We're not going,' she said desperately.

'Your sister wants you at her wedding whatever you're wearing. Green's not your colour anyway. It doesn't suit you.'

Kirstie sat in the car, the wet dress creasing into heavy folds round her thighs and across her stomach. She was too unhappy to protest any further. She did not care what happened.

Carson drove away quickly after consulting a map. A few miles further on, he took a slip road off the motorway, driving through agricultural land and pretty Warwickshire villages.

'Keep your eyes skinned,' he said.

'What for?'

'A shop.'

Carson saw it first, a small country boutique, half hidden in a sleepy, tree-lined square. There were only two elegant models in the window, and they shouted expensive. One was a skinny white dress with brief, cutaway jacket and a huge, cartwheel red straw hat.

'That one,' he said.

Ten minutes later, Kirstie was wearing the outfit, dazed and bemused by the speed of the transaction. The white dress fitted like a dream, the short skirt showing off her shapely legs, the jacket madly fashionable with detailed seaming that was reflected in the price. Carson took down a white silk teddy from a rail, knowing she would hate to be wearing stained underwear, and handed it to her. He paid by cheque while she changed.

'I'll pay you back, of course,' she said.

'Marry me instead. Why not? I'm always buying you clothes.'

He tossed the hat into the back of the car and grinned at her. 'Only joking. But you do look stunning—enough to go to any man's head. How about one of your Grade A smiles?'

Suddenly her spirits soared and she threw caution out of the window. 'A smile and a kiss,' she said, planting a warm kiss on his smooth cheek. She didn't care what he thought of it. This was her sister's wedding day; she was with Carson, the man she loved, and she was going to enjoy every minute.

They made a sensational entrance at the church, Carson, so tall and splendid-looking in his grey suit, his assurance and charm taking him easily through all the introductions. Kirstie looked elegant in her expensive white outfit, the red straw the perfect frame for her silvery hair.

'Hello, Mum,' she said, holding on to the brim as she bent to kiss her mother.

'You're here, Kirstie,' said Mrs Duvall, her eyes already moist with the emotion of the occasion. 'And you look lovely.'

Kirstie hardly recognised Sean. Surely that fresh-faced young man in an obviously new suit was not the reason for her months of hurt pride? The features she had carried around in her mind had been quite different, older and with more character. But there was no time to ponder on this strange discovery before the organ broke into triumphant peals and Kate appeared, all frothy and radiant, her white lace dress swirling round her.

Kirstie felt a catch in her throat, moved beyond words. It was not only seeing Kate so pretty, but also seeing her father, pride on his ageing face as he led his daughter down the aisle.

The words of the marriage service were suddenly full of meaning. Kirstie was acutely aware of Carson standing beside her, his sleeve occasionally brushing her arm. His light baritone joined in the hymn-singing with an uncertainty in some notes which was endearing. She could not look at him, knowing her face would give her away.

The ceremony moved onwards: the signing of the register, the procession of bride and groom followed by the blushing bridesmaids. Sean's eyes momentarily lit up when he saw her. That was all. It was over in seconds.

Carson never left her side at the lakeside reception. It was as if he knew she was going through an ordeal and needed support. But as time went on, Kirstie realised that it was no ordeal. That New Year party had been nothing but a bit of fun.

'Our Kirstie, as gorgeous as ever,' said Sean, kissing her cheek heartily. 'I wondered if you'd come,' he added with a slight look of apprehension. It was as if he knew he had not played fair and felt guilty about it.

Kirstie was able to look him straight in the eye, seeing him as he really was. It was a moment of healing, a time to restore harmony.

'Kirstie always looks gorgeous,' said Carson, sliding his arm protectively round her slender waist. 'I've only once seen her looking like a stagnant pond.'

Kirstie almost choked on her champagne. Sean looked bewildered.

'I couldn't miss my own sister's wedding, now could I?' she said cheerfully. The Sean she had been fantasising about did not exist. He had been a figment of her imagination, a lover born out of her loneliness; she could dismiss him from her mind forever.

It was a perfect afternoon, with guests drifting about the lawn and down to the lakeside. Carson slung his jacket over one shoulder and Kirstie took off her high heels, letting the soft springy grass tickle her feet. They walked together, talking, but never mentioning AAMS. It was an unspoken pact not to spoil the day. Kirstie felt happier than she had done for a long while.

When the time came for the bride and groom to leave for their honeymoon in Wales, Kate took Kirstie aside and hugged her.

'It's been so wonderful to see you, having you here. You will come and stay, won't you? There's masses of room at the farmhouse.'

'You won't have time for visitors,' said Kirstie. 'You'll be too busy hand-rearing all those lambs.'

'Come anyway! Your midwifery will be useful.'

They laughed together and hugged again. Carson

was watching her, the look in his eyes unfathomable. Kirstie mistook it for an impatience to be going.

'We could leave now if you want to see your sister,' she suggested.

'You will come again, won't you, dear?' asked her mother. 'Bring that nice Dr Black. We've got a spare room now that Kate's flown.'

They slipped away, Kirstie quiet and thoughtful when the goodbyes were over. There was so much to think about on the drive to Carson's sister's home. It had been an unnatural day and Kirstie wanted to relax, to take stock of her future, plan her next move.

Carson put the Lotus into a low gear as the car bumped down a narrow rural lane, banks of wild lupins and blackberries hiding the hedgerows. He turned the car into a cobbled courtyard and several cats ran for their lives. Two dogs started barking and wagging their tails. A tall, coltish girl ran out of the cottage and flung herself into Carson's arms.

'Oh, Carson! Carson, at last! You've come. Have you brought Rauza for me?'

'Still useless at maths. Can't you even count to six? No, it's not time to bring Rauza yet, but I will. This time I've brought Kirstie. Kirstie, this is my sister, Grace.'

Kirstie found herself looking into the same intense blue eyes, yet these were veiled and vulnerable. The girl's dark hair was tied back in a pony-tail, but there was no mistaking the face and the features. This was the girl in the framed photograph in the hallway of Carson's home. Not a wife, but a sister.

The last shred of strain rolled away. Kirstie's smile was wide and happy. She held out her hand.

'Grace. . . I'm glad to meet you.'

'I thought Carson was bringing me a lost waif,' Grace laughed.

'A waif, but not lost,' said Carson abruptly. 'Kirstie knows where she's going—at least, I think she does.'

At first glance, Kirstie thought Grace was younger than Carson, but gradually she realised that the pony-tail, the exuberant greeting, the non-stop chatter were not signs of youth but part of a charade. Grace had streaks of grey in her hair and crowsfoot lines crinkling her eyes.

It was a picturesque and rambling cottage, overflowing with various cats and dogs, flowers and plants. Grace made a precarious living drying flowers and herbs which she sold to craft shops and at markets. Her kitchen was hung with bunches of drying blooms.

'Tea!' Grace announced. 'Home-made scones, home-made raspberry jam, lashings of cream. Come on, tuck in.'

'We've just been to a wedding reception, girl!' Carson groaned.

'But a cup of tea would be lovely,' said Kirstie.

By the time Kirstie unpacked in the tiny rose-sprigged guest-room that evening, she felt she had known Grace for years. Something about the woman was so appealing. She had all of Carson's charm, but none of the power and authority. And Carson was so different, listening to his sister's chatter with lazy affection, his eyes rarely leaving her face.

'Make him come more often,' said Grace, as if Kirstie had some say in Carson's activities. 'He works far too hard.'

'I know he does,' said Kirstie.

'She only wants me to give her cats their injections and clean out their ears,' Carson grinned. 'She seems to think I'm a vet.'

'Doctoring animals is nearly the same as people,' said Grace.

'There are a few basic differences, dear sister. Anatomy for a start, and the ability to communicate symptoms.'

'But my cats do communicate,' Grace insisted, a large mackerel tabby purring into her ear. 'Listen to this.'

'Translate.'

'He's saying he loves me.'

'Very useful,' said Carson drily.

Grace stood up, the cat still in her arms. 'Well, goodnight, you two. Lock up, will you, Carson? I still keep country hours.'

Kirstie smiled her goodnight, wondering how she could escape being left alone with Carson. The only way was to go. But Carson stopped her, effectively blocking the doorway with his tall frame.

'Don't go,' he said. 'Stay and talk. You've been very distant all day.'

'Distant? Hardly, Carson. I've been your shadow, quiet and polite, the perfect companion.'

'I don't want you quiet and polite. I want the sparky tiger woman. You're allowed to say what you think when we're not on duty. Now's your chance. Grace obviously thinks we want to be alone.'

'And we don't, do we?' said Kirstie, backing off.

'Maybe you don't, but I do. Sit down, woman, and stop prowling. You're making me nervous. How about this chair? Far enough away from me to suit you? I notice you're treating me as if I were contagious.'

'I just think we've done all the talking necessary,' said Kirstie with a hunted look. 'I'm very grateful to you for today, for coming to Kate's wedding. It doesn't mean that you have to make conversation or treat me any differently from the way you have in the past few weeks.'

'So how have I treated you in the past weeks?' he asked, leaning back, linking his hands behind his head. Kirstie could not see the expression in his eyes or tell if he was teasing or being coldly clinical.

She perched on the arm of the sofa to show that she was not staying. If he didn't know, then she would tell him.

'Cool, distant, unsympathetic, critical, superior, aggravating, scornful——' she began vehemently.

'Hold on, before you throw the entire book at me! Those words describe exactly your attitude to me since you gave in your notice. Perhaps you allow yourself to act any way you like, but I'm not permitted the same leeway. Isn't that crass hypocrisy?'

'That's not true,' said Kirstie wretchedly. 'Look, it's been a long and difficult day and I really can't cope with any more of it. I'd like to go to bed and wake up and find it's tomorrow.'

'My sentiments exactly,' Carson said wickedly. 'Your bed or mine?'

She made to move quickly, forgetting she was balanced on the arm of the sofa. As she slipped, he leapt from his chair and caught her, sweeping her into his arms and back on to the cushioned length of the sofa. He smothered her into a long, passionate embrace that took her breath away, his mouth silencing her protests.

Kirstie felt the most wonderful exhilaration as their bodies melded against each other. It was too late to stop his kisses. She had no power, no control. She just gave herself up to the inexorable pleasure that he knew how to give.

He shifted off her, reluctantly, leaning on one

elbow. He pushed her dishevelled hair off her face and kissed the end of her nose.

'I never did get to kiss the bride,' he complained vaguely.

'Will the bride's sister do?'

'More than adequately. But in the interest of Grace's sofa, moral propriety and other considerations, perhaps we should both retire to our separate beds.'

He gazed down at her, trying to learn something from the glowing expression on her face. She was all soft and womanly, her glossy look replaced by a dewy loveliness.

'Yes, Doctor,' said Kirstie, unsure if she was thankful for the reprieve or not.

They were halfway back to London when the car telephone rang, a feeling of urgency in its strident tones. Carson slowed down before picking up the receiver.

'Carson Black,' he said. He nodded a few times as he listened. The scrambled voice at the other end sounded like Lynda, high-pitched and anxious.

'Don't worry, Lynda. Put through a request to air brokerage for a BAC 1–11 and see how many stretchers can be fitted. Sister Duvall? Yes, I know where she is.' He shot a quick glance at the still woman at his side. Kirstie already understood the impact of his instructions. 'Get two more freelance nurses, a locum, and arrange to come yourself. We'll be at Heathrow in two hours.'

He put the receiver back on its cradle. Kirstie waited for him to speak. She could sense his brain running through a dozen alternatives.

'That's the end of your weekend, Kirstie. This is a

big emergency. At least eleven seriously injured and elderly passengers from one of those Mediterranean cruises. There was a bad storm at sea and a lot of passengers got thrown about. The ship was damaged and is limping into Port Mahon on the island of Minorca. There's a deep natural harbour and plenty of shelter. We should be in Mahon before it arrives. The small hospital in the port will be overwhelmed.'

'Are you planning two-tiered stretchers? And we'll need wheelchairs. Some may be walking cases.'

'These elderly people go on cruises thinking it's safe and easy on board ship. They forget about the pitch and toss, negotiating gangways and steep steps, the stormy seas of the Bay of Biscay. And this'll be your swan-song,' Carson added, being deliberately tactless. 'I checked your work sheets with AAMS. You're owed some holiday time.'

The last time of working with Carson. For a moment Kirstie felt physically sick. Physician, heal thyself, she challenged, and she would, she would.

'Your sister is a lovely person,' she said, changing the subject. 'I saw her photograph in the hallway of your house.'

She waited to see if Carson volunteered any further information, but the grave expression on his face did not change.

'That was taken several years ago,' he said, after a pause.

'You were holding a child in the photograph, a little boy. I—I thought he was your son.' She saw a tightening of Carson's mouth and wondered if she had ventured too far into the privacy which he guarded so fiercely.

'That was Timmy, Grace's son,' he said.

'Grace's son. . . I didn't realise she was married,'

Kirstie prattled on. 'He looks a lovely youngster. I suppose he's at school now?'

Carson checked the rear-view mirror and began manoeuvring the powerful car into the nearside lane. 'Five-minute pit stop for coffee,' he said, not answering her question. 'It'll have to be quick.'

They found a clean table in the cafeteria at the next service station, bought coffee, sipped the first reviving mouthfuls. Carson regarded the sweet, delicate face opposite him, her dark lashes curled thickly against her soft cheeks as she drank. He was sorry he was going to bring sadness to those expressive hazel eyes. He knew exactly how she would react.

'I think perhaps I should tell you about Timmy and Grace,' he began.

Kirstie shook her head. 'You don't have to.'

'You wouldn't think from that photograph that Timmy had a shaky start in life. He was born with cardiac deformities which gave him no chance of survival if untreated. Grace and Tom agreed to a two-hundred-to-one surgical procedure at Killingbeck Hospital,' he said.

'Killingbeck is an excellent hospital,' said Kirstie, wishing now that she had never mentioned the little boy.

'It was a seventeen-hour operation, working on a tiny heart the size of a walnut,' said Carson, remembering the crowded operating theatre, the tense but calm atmosphere, his diminutive nephew as still as a doll.

'You were there?'

'Yes. Timmy had truncus arteriosus, which requires the most complicated surgery. Grace wanted me to be there. The surgeon was a brilliant man and I did little more than assist. He re-routed the blood vessels, replaced a missing part of the aorta with a graft and repaired a hole by sewing in a patch.'

'Amazing,' said Kirstie, full of admiration and awe for the skill of today's surgeons. 'Little Timmy was lucky.'

'It was the longest day of my life,' said Carson, his thoughts still far away. 'Somehow Timmy pulled through. It was quite remarkable to see that little mite battling for life. He wasn't going to let go without a fight.'

Kirstie smiled at Carson, but his eyes were riveted on her and she already sensed that her enthusiasm was out of place. She reached across the table and touched his hand tentatively.

'Carson? What is it?'

'Eighteen months later the hole repair was damaged by infection. These things happen. It's not possible to prevent everything. Timmy needed a second major open-heart operation. It lasted three and a half hours. Complications set in and, though at first we thought he was going to make it, the struggle was too much. Six days later he died.'

The anguish in his voice, the grimness on his face told Kirstie all she needed to know. He had loved that little boy as if he were his son. Now she understood his tenseness while caring for Baby Wallace; he had been reliving those traumatic months with Timmy.

'I swore then I'd never marry, never have children, never put a woman through the same suffering that Grace endured. It nearly killed her—all the months of worry, and then losing him anyway. Tom couldn't cope. It broke up their marriage and she's on her own now. I ought to go and see her more often, but it only reminds me of Timmy. I'm too much of a coward.'

He looked up, saw Kirstie's stricken face and caught

at her hands. 'Oh, I'm so sorry, my dear—I didn't mean to upset you. I should have known. You've helped us both this weekend, talking to Grace and by just being there. I haven't seen Grace looking so natural and happy with anyone for a long time. It was a very pleasurable visit, not morbid or miserable, and it was all due to you.'

'You're not a coward, Carson,' said Kirstie, slipping her fingers between his. 'Never, never. It's a very normal reaction to bereavement, keeping away, pretending it hasn't happened, burying oneself in work. I'm so dreadfully sorry about your dear little nephew, but he survived for far longer than expected, and I expect he had a really happy and much loved family life with loving parents and a doting uncle. He had no chance at all when he was born, had he? Before all these modern surgery techniques, he would have died quite naturally. As for never marrying or never fathering a child yourself. . . You can't make that kind of decision so coldly. There might be some woman somewhere who would disagree with you. Perhaps it's a risk she'd be prepared to take. . .for the sake of loving you.'

'You're very good to be with,' he said, with a sudden heart-stopping smile. 'I like being lectured by a pretty blonde. Drink up, we ought to go now.'

Kirstie seethed momentarily. She hated being called a pretty blonde, but she realised Carson was only using the phrase to defuse the emotion of the moment. She turned away, retrieving her handbag.

'Second lecture at three p.m.,' she said. 'Subject: Medical Men and Manners, Part Two.'

'I'm glad I skipped Part One,' he said.

They made good time to the AAMS offices. Lynda raised her eyebrows at Kirstie's white outfit and big straw hat. Kirstie did not realise that a few petals of confetti still clung to the red straw.

The big BAC 1–11 stood waiting on the tarmac, gleaming aluminium and steel, belly doors open. Technicians were bolting two-tiered stretchers into place along each side of the cabin. Equipment was being trundled aboard, oxygen cylinders, resuscitation units; the plane was being converted into a complete intensive care unit.

Lynda was in her element, bustling about, ordering the crew around like a lot of junior nurses. She was not wearing the new uniform but had reverted to the traditional stiff navy dress and starched cuffs.

'It'll be warm in Minorca,' Carson warned her as they checked on the progress of equipping the plane.

'I don't approve of nurses in trousers,' she sniffed. 'It doesn't look right. These patients will be elderly people and they'll expect a nurse to look like a nurse.'

'How is it that you disapprove of the new uniform so whole-heartedly, when you were the one who designed it?' Carson asked.

Lynda flushed. Her face gave her away. She shot a quick look at Kirstie, hoping to bluster her way through the silence, but Kirstie refused to come to her rescue.

'Well, it seemed expedient at the time,' she said lamely.

'No need to explain further,' said Carson. 'I believe I may have been blind—another of my faults.'

Kirstie caught the merest glimmer in his vibrant blue eyes. There was no need for any explanations. He understood.

It was a strange take-off in the big laden carrier after the small, zippy executive jets. Kirstie felt she ought to be handing out duty-free or checking seatbelts. The two freelance nurses, Ruth and Jane, were also finding the extra space a novelty.

'We're going to see a lot of fractures, broken hips, severe loss of blood. Many of these old people won't be fit to move yet. We may have to make two trips. I'll know better when I've made my assessments, but be prepared for a long mission,' said Carson, stretching out his legs and half closing his eyes.

But he could still see Kirstie and her silvery hair shining like a halo, and suddenly he knew he had been incredibly blind.

# CHAPTER TEN

MINORCA came into sight, a windswept island, a lozenge of lush greenness, the northern coast with dramatic cliffs dropping into the blue Mediterranean. It was not mountainous like Majorca, its highest point being the hill-sized Monte Toro.

Kirstie glimpsed the crippled cruise liner limping towards Port Mahon and thought of all the distressed and injured passengers aboard. She wanted to reassure them: we're here, we're coming. The deep inlet of Port Mahon was dotted with ships of all kinds, white houses spilling down the steep hillsides to the harbour. She knew Lord Nelson had once been stationed there and had shared a house called Golden Farm with Lady Hamilton.

The hospital was near the main shopping centre and stadium in Mahon. It was sparkling clean, cool and airy, a hive of activity. Preparations were going ahead for the huge influx of casualties; several doctors on holiday had turned up, hearing of the emergency on the radio.

Carson immediately got into radio contact with the ship's doctor, a young man, recently qualified, who seemed quite astonished to have so many patients.

'They were falling about like ninepins,' he said over the loudspeaker.

'Well, they would be, wouldn't they, if the ship was rolling?' said Carson. 'Can you give me any details of the injuries?'

'Hold on a minute.' They heard a prolonged rustling

175

of papers and Kirstie had to laugh at the stoic expression on Carson's face. 'Right now, I've got them.'

'Take your time,' said Carson in his most laconic manner. 'You aren't trying to beat the clock.'

'Yes, sir. Now, we've two broken hips, one of whom needs cardiac care. An ECG and rhythm strip have been evaluated, but of course you'll need to check the location of the peripheral oedema and the quality of heart and breath sounds before making a decision.'

'Naturally,' said Carson.

'We have a displaced fracture of the pelvis on pain-relievers only. Urinary catheter in place, draining not closed off. He needs checking for internal injuries.'

Carson shot a placid glance at Kirstie. 'This young man will go far,' he murmured. 'Textbook perfect!'

'An elderly woman has broken both wrists, quite a mess. There's a man with a smashed nose and a lot of facial cuts. You should watch out for epistaxis which could be troublesome in flight. If possible, I'll remove the nasal packs, or just before take-off you could cauterise the bleeding points. Or you could try bilateral nostril compression if we can't control the bleeding.'

Kirstie hid her amusement at Carson's pained expression. 'Does the patient with the broken nose have to come home right away? The pressure change at altitude on ears and sinuses could be a problem,' she said.

Carson relayed the question to the ship's doctor.

'Yes, he does want to come home,' the young man replied. 'The woman with the two broken wrists is his wife. One break is a complicated fracture and needs resetting with steel pins. Naturally they want to stay together.'

'They'll be sorry they didn't go to Eastbourne,' joked Carson.

'They live in Eastbourne.'

The list was long and complicated. Kirstie and Lynda made their own notes; so many of the patients would need extra care. They were in for a long, hard haul.

The AAMS team helped with the work in the hospital, moving and making up beds, sterilising dressings and instruments, making arrangements for extra drugs and food. They waited for the cruise ship to arrive, but daylight was fading before they heard of the delay.

'Two tugs are needed to bring the cruise ship up the deep and narrow three-and-a-half-mile inlet,' said the hospital registrar, Dr Camacho. 'One of them has engine trouble. It will be another couple of hours at the earliest. I'll make arrangements for your team to have somewhere to sleep,' he added courteously.

'That's very kind,' said Carson. 'Much appreciated.'

'Senior sisters will sleep in the staff-room,' Lynda decided. 'Armchairs will do for us.'

Carson took Kirstie's arm and nodding to the others, headed for the corridor. 'I think a breath of fresh air is in order while we've time.'

Port Mahon had become a series of twinkling lights up the hillside; people were strolling along the quay-side which was connected to the town by flights of steps, holiday-makers enjoying the faded Georgian architecture, picturesque archways and wrought-iron balustrades.

'How thoughtful of Lynda to allocate me an armchair,' said Kirstie.

'You're going to sleep in the Caves of Xoroi, that is if the ghost of Xoroi doesn't disturb you.'

'I'm supposed to sleep in a cave?' Her voice rose, even more astonished.

'The sound of the seas below will rock you to sleep,' said Carson mysteriously. 'Change out of your uniform and I'll drive you there. Nowhere is far on this island. Dr Camacho says it's only fifteen minutes.'

'This is crazy,' she murmured, slipping into the staff cloakroom. She had packed the white wedding outfit into her overnight bag as there had been nowhere suitable to leave it on the reorganised BAC 1–11. It seemed so strange to be changing back into the striking dress. She had never thought she would wear it again so soon.

The night was still warm as she went outside the hospital and found Carson waiting in a sardine-sized Fiat. There was hardly room for his long legs to work the pedals.

'Kindly loaned by Dr Camacho. Now you know why I run a Lotus,' he said, crashing the gears as he reversed the unfamiliar car outside the hospital yard.

'Are you having me on?' Kirstie asked. 'Is this some kind of juvenile joke? I don't think we should leave the hospital. Do you know where we're going?'

'Cala 'n Porter,' he said. 'Stop worrying. I've got a map and I'll phone every half-hour.'

'If I'm not back in time I'll get the sack,' she said without thinking. They both burst into laughter and some of her tenseness left her. She would leave it to Carson. If he made her late, it was entirely his responsibility.

They drove past isolated villages built in desolate scrubland and hilly countryside. Cart tracks radiated from the main road to more inland hamlets. Carson turned down a rutted dirt track with masses of potholes that shook the little car from side to side.

'Are you sure this is the right road? You didn't mention an obstacle course,' said Kirstie, clinging to the seat.

'Dr Camacho warned me. It's nearly over.'

The road suddenly changed to a good metallic surface and they passed some of the strange ancient monuments called taulas, huge T-shaped stone edifices that had their beginnings in unrecorded time.

'Fascinating,' said Kirstie, as they stopped briefly to look at one by the roadside. The pitted grey stone stood sentinel to its secrets.

'Some people think they were the central pillar of a big communal building. Or they may have a religious significance.'

'I love old things,' said Kirstie.

'I suppose that's why you manage to get on with Lynda,' said Carson. He coloured slightly under his tan as Kirstie's mouth broke into a wide smile.

'Now who's busting the protocol rule?' she teased. 'Weren't you taught as a student to be deferential to matrons?'

'Sorry, Sister. Spoke without thinking.'

Kirstie knew there had been a lot of personal healing for her in going to Kate's wedding and that visiting his sister had been good for Carson. Now this unconventional doctor was taking her to some cave, and instead of trusting him she was all on edge.

Cala 'n Porter was a deep cove between rocky headlands that towered above a sandy beach. The hillside was polka-dotted with dozens of tiny white cottages that clung to the rockface as if by magic.

'One of those villas is my bed for the night,' said Carson. 'Villa San Luis—if I can find it. Dr Camacho lets it out as a holiday villa and it's empty at the moment.'

'How kind. You get a villa and I get a cave. There's equality for you!'

'Caves are ideal for mermaids.'

Carson seemed to know where he was going, though Kirstie was getting more and more anxious. He took a road towards the high cliffs and turned into a car park overlooking the sea.

'The Caves of Xoroi,' he announced, opening the passenger door and helping Kirstie out. 'They were once inhabited.'

'Look, I think I'd rather stick with an armchair.'

He did not appear to be listening. He took her hand and led her towards a small entrance and they began to walk down a rocky path.

'Xoroi was a black slave who swam ashore from a pirate vessel and became a cave dweller. He fell in love with a village girl and took her back to the caves.'

'Is this my bedtime story?' Kirstie murmured as they entered the first of a long series of connecting caves. It was very eerie and strange; they were lit with lamps and candles on ledges, and far away in the distance Kirstie heard strains of music.

Carson nodded and ducked an overhanging rock. 'Understandably the villagers were pretty annoyed and chased Xoroi every time he came out to find food, but he knew this labyrinth so well they could never find a way in.'

He stopped at a small admissions desk and bought vouchers for drinks. It was still very dark, but their eyes were becoming accustomed to the gloom. Kirstie's hand was safely tucked into Carson's and his closeness was warm and reassuring.

'One night it snowed, the only time it's ever snowed in Minorca. The villagers followed Xoroi's huge footsteps in the snow, found the girl and her baby sons, and carried them back. When Xoroi discovered that all his family had gone, he was so distraught he ran to the edge of the caves and jumped to his death in the seas below.'

They paused at a jagged gap and looked down at the dark, foaming seas pounding the rocks. It was a very long way down. Kirstie shivered. She could imagine the poor slave's distress when he knew he had lost the family he loved.

'Some bedtime story,' she said. 'Guaranteed to make me sleep.'

'Could you really sleep with this racket going on?'

The music had grown in volume. They reached a much larger cave filled with people dancing and sitting at little tables with candles. Shadows flickered on the rockface walls as bodies writhed and cavorted to the latest pop.

Carson bent to speak close to her ear. 'You've been hinting for weeks about going dancing,' he said with unashamed exaggeration. Kirstie smiled, thankful she did not have to answer. He was so unexpected. Life with Carson would be full of surprises. But she was leaving him and this would be her true swan-song. She pulled him towards the dance-floor.

'Sorry, I can't do this,' he laughed. 'I'll just stand and look interested.'

But he moved in a lanky, economic way in time with the music, and Kirstie's heart filled with love for him, catching his hands, then losing them, her own dancing sending messages of primeval longing across the space between them.

The music changed to something slow and quiet, and Carson fetched two long drinks from the bar. He drew her away into another smaller cave and set the drinks on to a tiny ledge.

'Kirstie, am I ever going to convince you that drug companies are not the big bad wolves of medicine? Thornhill ploughs back a high percentage of its profits into research.'

'Are we going to talk shop when there's all this lovely music?' Kirstie could not help swaying to the pulsing rhythm.

'Don't change the subject, and stop looking so gorgeous. You're ruining my line of thought and we're fast running out of time. One of my programmes at Thornhill is extended clinical trials to find the under-lying cause of Myalgic Encephalomyelitis.'

'Post-Viral Fatigue Syndrome or ME,' said Kirstie, wishing he would just dance.

'What do you know about it?'

She sighed. 'It's a mysterious disease with long and debilitating fatigue, CNS disturbance with headaches, dysphasia, mental incapacity and paraesthesiae.'

'We think it's a disorder of the fatty metabolism following a viral infection. We're monitoring four hundred patients all round the country, giving half a dietary supplement of essential fatty acids and the other half a placebo.'

'How long will the trials take?' Kirstie asked, interested despite her longing to dance.

'Seven months. Every patient is monitored, recorded, facts fed into a computer, results evaluated. We're hoping that the patients on the supplement may have benefited. Now, do you really think I'd be better occupied fixing some woman's ingrowing toenails?'

'But where did the profits come from in the first place?' Kirstie insisted. 'From other patients, of course, desperately ill people.'

Carson touched her face with a fingertip. 'I don't think I'm ever going to win this argument.'

'You could dance with me instead,' she said softly, drawing him back on to the dance-floor. 'That rates several house points.'

Going into his arms was like an electric shock. For a moment neither of them could move, memory cells reliving other embraces. Carson was so right for her in every way, Kirstie despaired. Why was she leaving? Why was she acting like a total fool, denying everything her body longed for? His hand went to the vulnerable curve of her neck, drawing her closer as they began to move to the slow seductive music. She breathed in the husky scent of his skin, drawing it into her body so that she would never forget.

They danced in a dream, not speaking, letting the music speak for them. Streaming stars were spiralling in Kirstie's mind as she gave herself up to the music, not caring if she betrayed the way she felt. Her hand slid upwards to rest on Carson's chest.

'Kirstie. . .Kirstie,' he breathed into her hair, holding the small of her back against him. 'What are we going to do about us? You can't go. . .'

Kirstie did not know if she really heard the words or if they were just echoes in her mind. The music was like a drug, invading her thoughts, creating an irresistible desire. Now they were playing 10CC's 'I'm not in love' and the poignant words shattered the last of her defences to the wanton feelings in her body. She curled her arms round his neck, fitting herself against him like a glove, her cheek touching his roughened chin.

'It's just a silly phase. . . I'm going through,' he sang, his mouth close to her ear. 'Kirstie. . .what more can I do? I'm going crazy trying to prove to you that I'm not a medical director with his mind solely on the profits. Not even a chief medical officer who thinks the pretty nurses are perks of the job. I love you. I want you. I want you to marry me.'

Kirstie stumbled in his arms. 'Marry me?'

They stopped dancing and stood together in the middle of the crowd, arms entwined, their eyes hungry with love. In the flickering darkness, Carson looked more like the handsome pirate of Agra, his firm chin shadowed, his indigo eyes dark and glowing. The suave doctor had momentarily disappeared.

'I want to marry you,' he repeated. 'I want to spend my life buying you clothes, and making sure you eat properly and get enough sleep.' With a laugh, he brought her back into his arms and touched her lips with a light kiss. 'Take a chance, Kirstie. Don't always play safe.'

'But only this morning, it was you saying you'd never marry, never have children——'

He silenced her with another kiss. 'I was a fool. I've done a lifetime of thinking since then. Please don't go.'

'I was only going because I couldn't cope with seeing you every day and loving you and knowing it was all hopeless,' said Kirstie in a great rush.

'But it isn't hopeless. It's going to be perfect. We can sort everything out. If we really love each other, then nothing is insurmountable. There are no barriers. Do you love me?'

'I do, I do, I do. . .' Kirstie whispered to herself.

'I fell in love with you the moment I saw you at Agra, hair blowing all over the place, shoes off, buttons undone. . . It was all I could do to keep my hands off you, there and then. But you so obviously disliked me and everything I stood for. What could I do in the face of such opposition? Every move I made was wrong. If you turn me down now, I'll probably jump from the cliffs like poor Xoroi.'

Kirstie gripped his arm with mock alarm. 'Don't do that. Please don't become a legend—I need you too much.'

'You need me? Now there's a joke. I've never met such an independent woman!'

'Carson, what a pair of fools we've been!' Kirstie said, overjoyed by the freedom to say exactly what she felt. 'I love you too, so much. It's been agony for me, trying to fight these feelings because of all my mixed-up ideas. I was out of my depth and I didn't want to get hurt.'

'If you love me, then why are you leaving me?' Carson's voice was both tender and angry. 'Why this ridiculous resignation?'

'I had to get away. . . I don't know.'

A small, wiry waiter hovered at Carson's side, unnoticed for some seconds. He coughed to attract their attention.

'*Perdóneme, señor el doctor*?' he said. 'Excuse me, the telephone, *por favor*.'

'Dr Camacho,' they said in unison.

'This way, *por favor*.'

They hurried to a phone booth hidden away behind the bar. Carson's conversation was brief.

'The liner will be docking in half an hour,' he said to Kirstie. 'Sorry to cut short the evening, but we'd better go.'

Kirstie accepted the disappointment but was radiantly happy just to be with Carson, his words still ringing in her ears, knowing that soon they would have time together, real time to get to know each other.

'Sorry, darling,' he said, kissing her fingertips. 'We'll have to continue this conversation later.'

'It can't be helped. Work comes first.'

'No, you come first, I promise you. Always. But when we've settled our patients, perhaps there'll still be some time for us.' He took a key out of his pocket, a questioning look in his smouldering eyes. 'The Villa San Luis?'

'What could be more perfect?' said Kirstie, her voice overflowing with love. His hands gripped her fingers with an urgency that conveyed all his love and care. It was a moment that neither would ever forget.

They arrived at Port Mahon in less than fifteen minutes. Kirstie ran into the hospital, changing quickly into her uniform while Carson shrugged into a white coat, checking his medical case and notes. Lynda Marshall was staying at the hospital, ready for the arrival of the patients.

'Nearly late,' she managed to say, disapprovingly.

'Almost early,' said Kirstie, waving as she flew through the door.

'Let's go down to the quayside and meet the casualties,' said Carson, opening the door of the Fiat. 'The ambulances are already there. The police have cleared the roads.'

The big white liner was anchored in deep water and a fleet of small motorboats was bringing the injured ashore. A stream of stretchers, wheelchairs and walking patients began to arrive. Carson and Kirstie exchanged a brief look before beginning their work. Among the first to be lifted ashore was a frail woman in a wheelchair, both arms in a sling, her face drawn with pain and worry.

'Mrs Newton?' said Kirstie, after consulting her list. 'How are you feeling? I'm Sister Duvall from the Air Ambulance Medical Service. I'm going to take care of you and help you get more comfortable. We'll be taking you to the hospital first.'

'It's all been quite dreadful, my dear. That storm was so frightening. But I'm so glad to see you and it's nice to be going home. You're a sight for sore eyes.'

'Isn't she just?' said Carson, coming round the other side of the wheelchair, his white coat flapping in the breeze, stethoscope in hand. His face was alive with love and pride, his eyes vibrant with desire. 'And, Mrs Newton, you're the first to share our good news. Sister Duvall has just agreed to become my wife.'

Despite her pain and discomfort, Mrs Newton was not slow. 'You didn't need to tell me that, Doctor,' she said. 'I could see it with my own eyes.'

Kirstie managed to look maidenly and modest, but professional at the same time. More passengers were coming ashore, some walking and some assisted by members of the crew.

'Do you mind, Dr Black?' she murmured. 'A little deference to a senior sister, please, while on duty.'

'I want the whole world to know. Mrs Carson Black. . .it sounds wonderful.'

'I said I'd marry you, but I didn't say I'd change my name,' said Kirstie with spirit.

'No,' Carson groaned, 'not another objection! Woman, it seems there's only one way to shut you up.'

He took her in his arms in front of a quayside crowded with casualties, passengers, crew, police, holiday-makers and local onlookers. They raised a small cheer, much to Kirstie's embarrassment.

'This will never do,' she said, straightening her uniform.

'I should think he'll do very nicely,' said Mrs Newton, smiling for the first time in days.

# 60th
# BEST SELLING ROMANCE

**THAI SILK – Anne Weale**                    **£1.45**

Anne Weale has been writing for Mills & Boon for 35 years. Her books are sold worldwide and translated into 19 different languages.
As a special tribute to Anne's success, Thai Silk, her 60th Mills & Boon Romance, has been beautifully presented as an anniversary edition.
An intriguing love story . . . Not to be missed!

**12th October, 1990**

*Available from Boots, Martins, John Menzies, W.H. Smith, Woolworths and other paperback stockists.*
*Also available from Reader Service, P.O. Box 236, Thornton Road, Croydon, Surrey, CR9 3RU.*

# A ROMANTIC TREAT FOR YOU AND YOUR FRIENDS THIS CHRISTMAS

Four exciting new romances, first time in paperback, by some of your favourite authors – delightfully presented as a special gift for Christmas.

**THE COLOUR OF DESIRE**
Emma Darcy

**CONSENTING ADULTS**
Sandra Marton

**INTIMATE DECEPTION**
Kay Thorpe

**DESERT HOSTAGE**
Sara Wood

For only £5.80 treat yourself to four heartwarming stories.

**Look out for the special pack from 12th October, 1990.**

*Available from Boots, Martins, John Menzies, W.H. Smith, Woolworths and other paperback stockists.*

*Also available from Reader Service, P.O. Box 236, Thornton Road, Croydon, Surrey, CR9 3RU.*

# IT'S NEVER TOO LATE FOR SWEET REVENGE . . .

Adrianne's glittering lifestyle was the perfect foil for her extraordinary talents. A modern princess, flitting from one exclusive gathering to another, no one knew her as The Shadow, the most notorious jewel thief of the decade. With a secret ambition to carry out the ultimate heist, Adriane had a spectacular plan – one that would even an old and bitter score. But she would need all her stealth and cunning to pull it off – Philip Chamberlain, Interpol's toughest cop and once a renowned thief himself was catching up with her. His only mistake was to fall under Adrianne's seductive spell.

**Published: October 12th**     **Price: £3.50**

# W RLDWIDE

*Available from Boots, Martins, John Menzies, W.H. Smith, Woolworths and other paperback stockists.*

*Also available from Reader Service, P.O. Box 236, Thornton Road, Croydon, Surrey, CR9 3RU.*

# Zodiac Wordsearch
## Competition

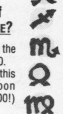

### How would you like a years supply of
### Mills & Boon Romances <u>ABSOLUTELY FREE</u>?

Well, you can win them! All you have to do is complete the word puzzle below and send it into us by Dec 31st 1990. The first five correct entries picked out of the bag after this date will each win a years supply of Mills & Boon Romances (Six books every month - worth over £100!) What could be easier?

| S | E | C | S | I | P | R | I | A | M | F |
|---|---|---|---|---|---|---|---|---|---|---|
| I | U | L | C | A | N | C | E | R | L | I |
| S | A | I | N | I | M | E | G | N | S | R |
| C | A | P | R | I | C | O | R | N | U | E |
| S | E | I | R | A | N | G | I | S | I | O |
| Z | O | D | W | A | T | E | R | B | R | I |
| O | G | A | H | M | A | T | O | O | A | P |
| D | R | R | T | O | U | N | I | R | U | R |
| I | I | B | R | O | R | O | M | G | Q | O |
| A | V | I | A | N | U | A | N | C | A | C |
| C | E | L | E | O | S | T | A | R | S | S |

| Pisces | Aries | Leo | Earth | |
|---|---|---|---|---|
| Cancer | Gemini | Virgo | Star | **Please turn** |
| Scorpio | Taurus | Fire | Sign | **over for** |
| Aquarius | Libra | Water | Moon | **entry details** |
| Capricorn | Sagittarius | Zodiac | Air | |

# How to enter

All the words listed overleaf, below the word puzzle, are hidden in the grid. You can can find them by reading the letters forwards, backwards, up and down, or diagonally. When you find a word, circle it, or put a line through it. After you have found all the words, the left-over letters will spell a secret message that you can read from left to right, from the top of the puzzle through to the bottom.

Don't forget to fill in your name and address in the space provided and pop this page in an envelope (you don't need a stamp) and post it today. Competition closes Dec 31st 1990.

Only one entry per household (more than one will render the entry invalid).

**Mills & Boon Competition**
**Freepost**
**P.O. Box 236**
**Croydon**
**Surrey CR9 9EL**

**Hidden message** _____

_____

**Are you a Reader Service subscriber.**   Yes ☐    No ☐

**Name**_____

**Address**_____

_____

_____

_____ **Postcode**_____

You may be mailed with other offers as a result of entering this competition.
If you would prefer not to be mailed please tick the box. No ☐          COMP9